Jack Spicer's
Detective Novel

The Tower of Babel

JACK SPICER'S
DETECTIVE NOVEL

THE TOWER
OF BABEL

Talisman House, Publishers

Hoboken, New Jersey

Published in the United States of America by

Talisman House, Publishers
Box 1117
Hoboken, NJ 07030

Manufactured in the United States of America
Printed on acid-free paper

Sections of this novel appeared earlier in *Caterpillar* (ed. Clayton Eshelman), *Mirage #4 / Period[ical]* (eds. Dodie Bellamy and Kevin Killian), *lift* (ed. Joseph Torra), *Aerial* (ed. Rod Smith), and *Poetics Journal* (ed. Lyn Hejinian and Barrett Watten). Manuel Brito's Zasterle Press in Tenerife printed chapter three as a chapbook. Talisman House and Lew Ellingham and Kevin Killian are grateful to these editors, and especially to Robin Blaser, literary executor for the Spicer Estate, for granting permission to publish this book, and for all his kindnesses. — Talisman is grateful to Lew Ellingham, Zoë English, Kevin Killian, and Gönül Uçele for their considerable assistance in preparing this edition of *The Tower of Babel*. — The drawing of Jack Spicer by Alice Notley is reproduced from Edward Foster's *Jack Spicer* (1991) with the permission of the publisher, the Western Writers Series.

Library of Congress Cataloging-in-Publication Data

Spicer, Jack.
    The Tower of Babel.
        p.   cm.
    At head of title: Jack Spicer's detective novel.
    ISBN 1-883689-05-8 (alk. paper) : $33.95
    ISBN 1-883689-04-X (alk. paper) : $12.95
    1. Authors, American—California—San Francisco—Fiction. 2. Gay men—California—San Francisco—Fiction. 3. San Francisco (Calif.)—Fiction.   I. Title.   II. Title: Jack Spicer's detective novel.
PS3569.P47T68   1994
813'.54—dc20   93-49854
                                                          CIP

Jack Spicer's
Detective Novel

The Tower of Babel

I

As good a place as any to start is with John James Ralston sitting almost alone and slightly drunk at three o'clock of a Thursday afternoon (the time of day is probably not accurate, the day of the week almost certainly is) at a small beer and wine bar called The Birdcage on the upper edge of Grant Avenue in San Francisco. The undeniables (those times that he later could not help remembering when other details were hazy or forgotten and, thus, the things, details, that must have been with him like invisible animals perched on his shoulder when the other details, the ones he had now forgotten or half remembered, happened just as importantly before him) were that he was in San Francisco for the first time in seven years, that his luggage was resting in three separate lockers in the Greyhound Bus Station, and that the emphatic but steady June sunlight of San Francisco was shining directly through the plate glass window of the bar into his eyes.

This somehow emphasized the strangeness. Bars in Boston (or, for that matter, bars almost anywhere) do not have plate glass windows. Rather, he thought, giving full consideration to the subject, they must have plate glass windows and then paint them black or red or something. He could remember bars with plate glass windows in Boston, but he could not remember the afternoon sun shining through them.

He signaled the bartender for another ale. The greenness of the bottle it came in somehow looked even more unfamiliar in the sunlight than the sunlight itself. But it shouldn't look unfamiliar, he thought, I used to drink it when I lived here. Did bars have plate glass windows when I lived here? He stopped the (half-amusing) train of thought and wondered — did they have plate glass windows when I lived here? No, he finally decided, not fully certain of the memory, I was twenty-three when I left here, I probably didn't go into bars on afternoons.

There are a thousand details Ralston was not able to remember from his first afternoon in The Birdcage. Did he look through the plateglass window at the people passing by on the street? Did he, if it really was three o'clock, watch the old Italian women out shopping for groceries, the Chinese children on their way home from school? Did he notice the mirror in the window in which one could watch, he did watch, people before they passed the window and after they left it?

A girl with a pimply face and horn-rimmed glasses spoke to him. Again a false, or at best, a reconstructed memory. Just as Ralston could not really remember what really happened when he took the train trip from Texas to California when he was three years old but had had to piece together the story of it from stories his mother had told him, half-memories, and sheer imagination, so it was here, so it was always with any process or person whose beginning when later remembered assumes importance. Whom did I first speak to in The Bird-cage he asked himself months later, and he conjured himself up an obvious composite, as patently artificial as a reconstruc-ted California mission, a girl with a bad complexion and horn-rimmed glasses who spoke to him:

"You look bored," she said. She looked directly, as if in excuse for her boldness, at the copy of *Partisan Review* which he had placed next to his ale glass on the bar.

"I was thinking of windows," he answered, startled enough, for he was not conscious that anyone was sitting beside him in the bar, to give an almost direct answer to the question. "About why they always paint windows in bars. Except here."

The girl giggled. In his reconstructed memory the giggle had more or less the sound of a fingernail scratched across a plate glass window. She remained silent, staring at his copy of *Partisan Review*.

He too remained obstinately silent. He had seen this girl in the Cafe Espresso houses in the Village when he was a gradu-ate student at Columbia, he had talked with her at all-night parties given at cold-water flats, and, on several dismal occa-sions, had gone to bed with her. When he left New York to teach in Boston he had found her in many of his classes (mak-ing a consistent and grubby B minus whenever he had any-thing to do about it) and several of her (a little older) were among his wife's best friends. He did not remember her in California, but he was twenty-three, he reminded himself again, when he left California.

The girl, by now his (reconstructed) memory pictured her as black haired and rather pudgy, got up from the bar stool and went to the jukebox. "I'll bet five to one that she plays a Miles Davis record," Ralston said to himself, almost out loud. She played a Miles Davis record. Pleased, for the first time since his plane had landed, he ordered another bottle of ale from the bartender although his glass was still half full. The girl stood by the jukebox swaying slightly and listening. Before the record was over she came back to the stool. She turned to him. "Mallarmé," she said, with the air of someone who was finishing a discussion.

For the first time Ralston began to realize that the ale was making his mind sluggish. This was all silly, a waste of the opportunity of first impressions. He should call up some of his old acquaintances, look in the phone book until he discovered one name that was there seven years ago which was still there, have dinner with this one and his new wife, or that one, who was suddenly bald, or that one, who had written poetry and now was selling office equipment. Anything was better than this hole in the memory, this passive self-indulgence.

The sunlight was glaring even more unemphatically through the window. He suddenly wanted to shout out to this ridiculous girl, to this ridiculous bar, regardless of consequences, "I am J. J. Ralston. A book of poetry of mine is reviewed in that magazine you're staring at. What do you think of that, you bitch?" Or should he leave this impossible bar (no more typical of the San Francisco he remembered than the window was), find a hotel room, get his bags out of the locker, have a quiet dinner, and go to sleep? Or should he have dinner first?

Instead of doing either of these things he bought a bag of peanuts from the bartender. They were unshelled and there seemed to be thousands of them in the package. He offered some to the girl who was still there, Ralston half suspected she would have disappeared during his train of thought, sipping slowly at her glass of dark beer. She nodded, swept a handful of the peanuts next to her glass, and thanked him.

"Everybody gives me peanuts," she continued morosely. "Other people they give beers to or even Bristol Creme sherry. Me they give peanuts." She made no effort to finish her beer as she might have if her intention was to have Ralston buy her another. She merely chewed peanuts and looked glum.

"I wasn't trying to be funny about the window," Ralston said. "It's what I was really thinking."

"Oh, I know you weren't trying to put me down," she replied. "That's why I said Mallarmé. You come from the East, don't you?"

"You know that from the way I talk?" Ralston ventured.

"No. From the suit. You can always tell by the suit." She closed her eyes for a moment. "Unless you borrowed it from somebody."

Ralston (and the ale) consented to the stereotype for the moment. "I'm from Boston," he said proudly, deciding to make the best imitation of Ivy League of which he was capable.

The girl's eyes again fell to the *Partisan Review*. "And you've come to dig the San Francisco Renaissance?"

This was a little too close to the truth. In a sense he had come to dig the San Francisco Renaissance. But the very recognizability was, as being recognized generally is, insulting and unfair. He examined his own weapons. He could pretend to be a reporter from an Eastern magazine and —

"You teach in a small college and write literary criticism," the girl was saying. "You used to write poetry but you gave it up after your wife had her first child."

Ralston felt absurdly pleased as one does when a perceptive stranger (she had scored so well on the rest of it) accuses you of the one fault of which you can not possibly be guilty. It brought him somehow a full acquittal of everything else. He put his hand on the copy of *Partisan Review* as if for support and said, "Actually I'm a pusher. I play the trombone and prefer men to women. I escaped from Boston with three sailors and six ounces of heroin."

She sat studying him for a minute. She nodded. "You may be a homosexual. You stopped writing poetry because you turned thirty."

Acquittal has to stop somewhere, Ralston thought. Even the fact that I still write poetry doesn't cover the fact that I have passed thirty. He wondered why he minded less about his wife and the literary criticism and the college. He lapsed into an offended silence.

"Am I right?" She was a little girl now, genuinely anxious to know how she had scored on the spelling test. She could not, Ralston figured her age at twenty-one, possibly imagine that the mention of his age depressed him.

"Why have I come out here to dig the San Francisco Renaissance?" he asked, half curious and half to postpone his inevitably qualified answer to her question.

"Because you want your heart back. Because you feel you lost something." She drank the rest of her beer in her enthusiasm. "Now, am I right? Now tell me, am I right?"

"You scored about fifty percent." Ralston became big brother now. It was the easiest thing to do. "I am married. I do teach in a small college. I do write some literary criticism. But I haven't stopped writing poetry and I don't have any children." He felt very proud to have said so little. She might even have heard of the poet J. J. Ralston, might even conceivably have read his book. He was dealing with her very fairly.

"That's more than fifty percent," the girl said.

"I suppose it is," Ralston replied. He signaled the bartender to refill the girl's glass. He now knew that he was going to tell the girl the full story of what had brought him to this dingy sunlit bar, knew it with the feeling of relieved inevitability that he had when he knew that he was going to get into a fight at a party, or pass out in fifteen minutes, or, merely, certainly, do something extremely foolish.

He looked at the girl. The new beer seemed to be as distant from her as the old one had been. "I used to live in California," he said. "I came back."

The bartender returned with his change. The girl remained silent, not even — as if she wanted to break the connection — eating his peanuts. But the decision was made. He had made scores of classes pay attention to stories far less interesting than the one he was about to tell.

"It was a football game," he said.

The girl looked puzzled.

"I think I came back to California because I watched a football game."

"It's the wrong season, isn't it?"

"It was last fall. I was watching my college playing another one, a traditional rival."

"What's the name of your college?" the girl asked.

"Pryce. You've never heard of it. It's just outside Boston. And the name of the other college was Grove Falls. That's in western Massachusetts."

The girl was silent. She had taken off her glasses and was polishing them with a rather grubby handkerchief. Ralston went on — certain now that he could not tell the story but more certain than ever that he had to tell it. "It was like any other football game, I guess. The point was what I started to think about while the game was going on." Impossible, he thought, meaning can't filter through embarrassment. "Grove Falls was beating the hell out of us. They were leading 24-0 at the beginning of the last quarter and then our team sent in a boy named Shay, a third-string quarterback."

"And Shay saved the day," the girl said.

"I know it sounds like that, but listen and you'll see what I mean. I can't even remember what happened in the fourth quarter, how the touchdowns were scored or anything like that. What I do remember is Shay, how he acted. He took the most incredible chances — passed from behind his own goal line, reversed his field three or four times on every running play — that sort of thing. When it was all over, Pryce had beaten them 28-24, beaten a vastly superior team. But that doesn't matter. What I'm trying to say is that I suddenly realized in that fourth quarter that I had never written a poem using the energy that they used, taking the chances that they took."

"You mean a poem about football?"

"No." Ralston was disappointed. His story wasn't coming through at all. "Football doesn't have anything to do with it. I mean pitting the energy, the chance-taking, or even a fraction of it against the eight-man line of language. What Shay was doing that afternoon was not human but not difficult either. I realized that I had never done it, but that I wanted to do it more than anything else in the world — and not with a football."

"So you burned all your previous poetry?"

"Of course I didn't. I had a book ready to come out. It's a good book. They are good poems. There are other ways to play football. Only —"

"Only?"

"Well, that's why I came to San Francisco this summer."

"I don't think you'll find many quarterbacks like that out here, but I wouldn't know," she said quietly. "By the way, what was Shay like in class?"

"Dull and unimaginative. The way good composers are. I taught English for one year at an academy of music and —" Now he had gotten the thing said (or the oversimplification of the thing said) he wanted to switch back gradually to polite, nonautobiographical conversation, but the girl refused to let him:

"And was your wife at this football game with you?"

"Forget it," Ralston said. "I just wanted to tell you why I came back to San Francisco." He turned, as rudely as he could not knowing quite what local conventions of rudeness would be, away and stared or pretended to stare through the plate glass sunlit window. That was another thing he could do. It would be seven or eight in Boston now. He could call Anne and tell her that he had arrived safely, or, since he never could really be sure when she did and when she didn't believe him, reassure her that he was really in San Francisco. She would be understanding. No, comfortable. No, disturbed about something that would have absolutely nothing to do with him like a translation of an article she had started since he left, or something she had read about atomic energy in a newspaper, or — And he would not be sure, never be sure whether she took this attitude to reassure him (as she might professionally pretend a vast unconcern to the hallucinations of one of the children she was treating) or whether it was merely, truly, a kind of gigantic absentmindedness which proceeded from the comfort of their love.

He turned back to the girl. "My wife's a psychiatrist," he said, feeling at the moment that this announcement was a kind of substitute for actually having made the call.

The girl looked down at the squirrel's nest of peanuts in front of her. He could see immediately that she felt she was being, what was it — put down, put on, put upon, that he was coming back from his wounds to attack her. "No," he said. "Really. She's a psychiatrist. A child psychiatrist. She treats

children. Mostly schizophrenic children. It's very interesting
work."

"And that's why your wife isn't with you?"

"Yes," Ralston said. "She has her own work." At the lie,
which was not really a lie because it was (barring the yes)
literally true, the whole scene of what Ralston had even before
it happened, been able to think of only as "telling Anne" came
suddenly, unbidden, to his ale-filled mind. One week and a
day ago (it was a Wednesday certainly, for his last final had
been on a Monday and he had had the last grades in on Tues-
day) one week ago last Wednesday and they had been sitting
(he in the comfortable chair and she on the couch that had the
glass coffee table) drinking their early evening martini, almost
ready to go out to the bad restaurant on Charles Street to
which they almost always seemed to go when neither she nor
he wanted to cook and neither he nor she wanted to make the
suggestion of a good restaurant to go to. She had just been
telling an elaborate but funny story about the struggle of Dr.
Birnbaum (of the second clinic not the first) to persuade her to
take her six-week vacation in September and October and not,
as they had planned, in July and August. Anne loved to tell
funny stories about her fellow psychiatrists — ones that (with
suitable adjustments here and there) would have fitted admi-
rably in the *New Yorker*. When, as he seldom did anymore, he
accused her of this (in one way or another), she would say in
perfect sincerity (in one way or another), "But Jim, I *like* the
New Yorker."

But this time he had shattered the anecdote, shattered it,
as he guessed, not more than a line from its climax. He had
put down his martini glass, empty, and said, "Anne, I can't
come to Paris with you."

He was sure that her first impulse was to nod her head or
to say, "You say you can't come to Paris with me —" She was,
as she would have pointed out, trained to react to shocking
statements that way. If she had that impulse, she suppressed
it. Instead, she put down her martini glass and said in a tense
and uxorious voice, "Why not?"

They had been planning to go to Europe that summer —
this summer, he amended, eight days ago. He was to spend
the last weeks of July and the first of August in Paris finish-

ing the biography of Emily Dickinson which he hoped would both get him an assistant professorship and help him lay to rest the ghost, that timid, vital ghost, that had haunted him since, in early adolescence with the help of Untermeyer's anthology, he had discovered poetry. Anne would be with him on and off, flitting to Psychiatric Congresses (or their equivalents) in places like Zurich and Antwerp and, finally, giving several lectures on American clinical methods at the Sorbonne where she had, only three years before, received her Ph.D. in Clinical Psychology. Then, in the remaining weeks of August, assuming their money would hold out as it was bound not to, they would go to southern France, Spain and/or Majorca. It was a ponderous plan, a farsighted one, one which could scarcely be destroyed by a mere sentence over an evening martini.

"Is it another thing like that Lambretta?"

The first summer of their marriage (and the second of his teaching at Pryce) he had suddenly bought a Lambretta and had cancelled their vague plans of a Canadian vacation with the announcement (just as blunt as this one — he supposed that psychiatrists, even wives that were psychiatrists, affected people that way) that he wanted to spend a part of the summer driving alone around New England with his Lambretta and a sleeping bag, that he wanted to learn what it was like to be Thoreau before he was too old to learn what it was like to be Thoreau. He broke his leg and his left arm, as she had told him he would, on the first week on a highway outside of Keene, New Hampshire, and Anne, who had been very very generous about it at the time, refraining even from telling it as an anecdote to her friends, nevertheless had, from time to time as the years passed, made use of the accumulated interest of this generosity.

"No. It is not like the Lambretta," he said and then began, with her help, an exchange of barbed witticisms, old accusations, even intimacies, that were repeated between them, almost ritually, on the occasion of every quarrel. There were set speeches on both sides, formal, and, in a way, reassuring. But they both knew that they were both, almost as a domestic unit, deliberately postponing the time that he would tell her the real reasons, the new reasons for his decision.

When he did finally state them, he stated them well. The football game (or rather the thought arising from the football game which had been, the word was almost festering, in his mind since the end of October) was not mentioned. He transposed. He had been reading Blake, he told her — into the figure of William Blake he managed to combine his reactions to Shay, the team itself, and the fourth quarter. It was a little literary, but Anne would not know that it was a little literary.

He went on to tell her that he was thirty-one and that his poetry, even though it had been published in *Hudson* and *Partisan* and *Kenyon*, and even though his book had received an excellent review from Randall Jarrell in the *New York Times Book Review*, was not poetry in the sense that a real or imaginary Blake's poetry was poetry — that it was not even just a qualitative difference (and this was easier to make clear than it would have been if he had talked about the fourth quarter but it was also less true) and that he had, while there might still be time, at least to make an attempt not to be what he had undoubtedly already become — an, face it, academic poet.

He was going to San Francisco for the summer, he told her. He was going to San Francisco exactly as a psychiatrist might go on a field trip to Uganda if he had heard of mysterious, miraculous cures being worked in schizophrenics by witch doctors. It was a wild goose chase, he told her, but perhaps the mere fact of its being a *wild* goose chase would have an effect on his poetry.

"But," she said, "I thought you told me —"

"I know," he said. "I think what I've read of the new San Francisco poetry is awful. I think that this talk of a Renaissance is a hoax dreamed up by that old charlatan Slingbot for the sole purpose of giving himself something to write about in the Eastern magazines. But I *know* where Paris ends, I *know* where New York ends, I *know* where Boston ends."

She agreed with him immediately. It was an excellent idea. He could stay the summer in San Francisco and perhaps work on the Emily Dickinson book if he didn't find the William Blake in himself that he expected to find. It would actually save money too. And she realized that she would be so busy in Europe —. Yes. And he could see her mind adjusting to the new circumstances almost thrilled that it had new circumstances to adjust to, like a steeplechase horse suddenly coming upon a new and unexpected fence. And he, of course, if he was robbed of the illusion that he was doing something impractical, something that could not be adjusted against, something, in short, that did not fit into the adult universe in which they both lived, if he was being robbed of this illusion by her practicality, let him be robbed now, at the start of the nonsense, before he had stored up too much imaginary wealth from this gesture, before he felt that his investment and the interest he drew from it were too precious to be surrendered to the blunt arms of common sense. In short, they went to dinner and discussed his plans for the summer.

But he was not at dinner. It was a week and a day later and he was in San Francisco. He had come upon no angels yet, had attempted to make no last quarter touchdowns, but he was here and ready. He began to feel exhilarated, giddy as if he were a seventeen-year-old alone in a new city, as if, to use the phrase that the seventeen-year-old would certainly use, he were on the edge of a new adventure.

While he and the girl had been talking a number of people had filtered into the bar, clustering mainly at the tables and talking fairly excitedly to each other — often as not without a single drink before them. Three of these — Ralston thought the word must be still "Bohemian" in the West — had come up to the bar and were talking to the girl next to him. They were quite a collection of types. The evident leader (or, at least, the person who was being followed as he went up to talk to the girl) was a tall thin Negro wearing horn-rimmed glasses who looked rather as Abraham Lincoln would have looked if Abraham Lincoln had been a tall Negro wearing horn-rimmed glasses. He now turned to Ralston. "This chick tells me you're a big daddy poet from the East. May we welcome you to The Birdcage?" He bowed deeply from his waist and his two companions began applauding. Several other people at different tables who could not have heard a word of the Negro's speech took up the applause.

Hostility, curiosity, or what, Ralston wondered. He rose from the bar stool and bowed quite as deeply to each of them. "I am very happy to receive your greeting."

"My name is Washington Jones," the Negro said. "May I present my two companions? This," he pointed to a young man in blue jeans and a T-shirt whose dirty blond curls came down almost to his shoulders, "is John Petersen, pride of Red Oak, Iowa, which itself is the home of radio station KICK, and this," pointing to the other young man, who was shorter than even Ralston's five foot eight, but with a fat baby face and closely cropped black hair, "this is Gregory Taxon, the famous painter of assorted insects and crustaceans. We are all interested in the contemporary arts."

Ralston bowed again. "As you must know," he said, "my name is W. H. Auden."

"No, man." The Negro smiling showed a set of teeth that did not, and Ralston could never figure out why they did not, look like Negro teeth. "No, daddy. You're not big and fat enough for that."

The one called Petersen with the long dirty blond hair had already picked up Ralston's almost empty ale bottle. He was looking at it with infinite sadness. "That green death can make you sick," he said in a high penetrating voice. "Drive you out of your skull," then bowing toward Ralston he put the bottle to his mouth and drained what was left in the bottle. "If you've got the bread," he added as if as an afterthought, "buy us a pitcher of beer and we can all drink."

"Mr. Petersen is inviting you to join us at our table," the tall Negro said. "And your young lady, of course."

There was no real rudeness to this, Ralston felt. It was more like an initiation, a rite of passage, or, more exactly, the horseplay indulged in when a newcomer on shipboard crosses the equator. Ralston signaled the bartender who was watching, neither amused nor concerned, and ordered a pitcher of dark beer. He purposely turned his back to everybody as he ordered it, looking directly, not even at the bartender, but at the sunlight, which was still streaming through the window. Was he being foolish, he wondered? Were these swans or geese he was inviting to this pitcher of beer? Every social system, every foreign Bohemia, has an aristocracy, a middle class, and a poor-white class, and a collection of people that don't belong, and, he was looking directly at the light now, travellers like me — who don't know at first which is which, who don't know what which class considers an insult and which an initiation, who don't know whether the girl and these three strange young men would be the equivalents in another environment of bankers, grocers, or cotton pickers, or are, and this was a frightening thought, equally strangers as himself. "You think too much about people," he told himself firmly and brought the pitcher of beer over to the waiting table.

The three already had glasses and began to pour the dark beer into them as soon as the pitcher arrived. Ralston noticed that the girl was still sitting at the bar. He got up again and came over to her. "Aren't you coming to the table?" he asked.

"No," the girl said, she already had the rest of the peanuts in front of her. "I've been there." Her voice was utterly final. Ralston paused a minute and then regretfully, as his one bridge into this world was broken, went back to the table. Composite figment of his aftermemory or real, Ralston never saw the girl again.

At the table the blond young man named Petersen was already pouring himself a glass of beer from the pitcher.

"l suppose you're from Flat Rock," the tall Negro said to Ralston as he sat down.

"Flat Rock?"

"Flat Rock College, man."

Ralston recognized the name. It was a small experimental college somewhere in the wilds of western Pennsylvania that gave no degrees, no credits, and, so far as Ralston knew, no courses. He had once met a painter who explained the system to him.

"I'm glad they're afraid to admit it now," Petersen said. "When they first started coming into town they boasted about it. Thousands of them in their beat-up Fords, their wives, their paintings, and their children. Real Grapes of Wrath scene."

"Flat Rock College," Ralston began.

"John is right," the tall Negro interrupted, "although he expressed himself somewhat hysterically. We in North Beach have been obliged to entertain a large number, but certainly not thousands, of refugees from this now unfortunately defunct educational institution. It has become almost natural to presume that any stranger we see is a Flat Rock kiddie. Of course," he interrupted himself by pouring a beer into his almost empty glass, "one could tell immediately by looking at your suit that you aren't one of them. Flat Rock clothes don't make it."

Ralston suddenly realized that he had had none of the beer himself. He reached for the pitcher to pour some into his ale glass, but, just as he was touching it, the so-far silent member of the trio grabbed the handle and quickly refilled his own glass.

The tall Negro pointed to him. "Gregory here is making it with a Flat Rock chick whenever he isn't painting pictures of insects. That is, he says he's making it with her."

The short boy's face broke into a pleasant foolish grin. "Sure," he said.

There was very little beer left in the pitcher. Ralston poured all of it into his glass. "I didn't know Flat Rock College had closed," he said. "When did all this happen?"

But it was as if the disappearance of the last beer in the pitcher had made him disappear also. The trio did not even ignore him. They merely started talking among themselves, sipping their beer slowly now, making allusive jokes among themselves in the latest fashionable language about how somebody had gotten into a fight with somebody over something, about how somebody else was going to leave town and whether he really was, even, and this was the only moment when Ralston was even faintly astonished, about a movie with Ava Gardner in it. Ralston thought as he sat there vaguely waiting for something to happen how well Lewis Carroll had described this kind of situation, the classic Stranger at a Table. Here was the Mad Tea Party. Washington Jones, if that really was his name, the Mad Hatter, John Petersen a rather fuzzy March Hare, and Gregory Taxon behind his pleasant foolish grin a Dormouse almost certain to be stuffed into the teapot (or the beer pitcher) at the end of the afternoon, and Ralston, a disenchanted Alice, who unlike his prototype had played the role often enough not to be puzzled or to ask questions about anything but not often enough not to be annoyed when questions, unasked, were unanswered. He was not going to buy them another pitcher of beer, even Alice had not been asked to bring her own tea with her, but he was not going to leave until he could appear, if only for a moment, in a less humiliating role.

So Ralston sat there, drinking his beer slowly as they drank theirs slowly because there was going to be no more beer, listening, he idly thought, as if he were not really listening to conversation but to a dull modern jazz record — the Mad Hatter an insinuating tenor sax, the March Hare a ragged trumpet, the Dormouse — no, he could not fit the Dormouse into that combo at all — he would have to be an oboe. Ralston had begun to wonder how an oboe would sound in a dull modern jazz record when he saw the door open.

This was one of the few things that Ralston later could be completely sure of. The girl might have been a composite; he had known Jones and Petersen and Taxon later and his memory of their conversation and their actions might have been based on how he knew, later, that they must have behaved then and not on how they actually did. But the figure now standing in the doorway, Ralston (the future Ralston that is) was sure he could remember in every detail and remember it accurately. There was no apparent reason for this since he obviously could not have known or even wildly guessed that the person framed in the doorway would have any importance to him in the future, any reason for remembering. As an example of this, he could not remember and, for that matter, she could not remember, except by reconstruction, by intelligent guessing, where he had first met his wife. But as he (the later Ralston again) remembered sitting in that chair facing the open door of The Birdcage, the buzz of the conversation (the alto sax was doing a solo about cowboy movies), the slant of the sunlight (which by now did not hit the bar at all but rather the floor below the bar), the real jukebox (which was two-thirds through Chet Baker's record of Funny Valentine), even the time which had been so inexact for the rest of the memory but which was now exactly (if one ignored the fact that bar clocks are always inaccurate) twelve minutes of five. It was ridiculous the motionlessness of this memory, and yet, in it, the figure came moving through the doorway.

First came the hands (as memory Picasso-like tried to reproduce in flat space the movement of his impression), thin enormous hands, and then the beer glass that the hands were

carrying, a different, larger beer glass than those used at The
Birdcage (logic told him that it must have been the beer glass
that located his attention to the hands — but no, the hands
came first). Framed behind the hands and the beer glass,
subsidiary for the moment, was the rest of the body, elongated
and gangling, a face in which he saw mainly curves and thin-
ness — and youth, of course, he must be only eighteen or
nineteen but that came behind the rest of it in the picture, a
corduroy jacket, huge faded khaki pants that came not quite to
his ankles and yet (he had no belt) were two sizes too large
for him at the waist. He was looking at Ralston too, curiously,
as if he were surprised that he too was making a permanent
recording of his impressions. There was no element of sexual
attraction, Ralston thought, in this exchange of, what was it,
recognitions, not even of the unidentified erotic which can
pass, unexpected and meaningless, between any two creatures
like a bolt of heat lightning in the summer sky. It was merely
— no, Ralston did not understand it then and remembering it
later he still did not, would not, understand it.

The others at the table now had seen him. "Rue," they
called. Unhurried and awkward he walked over to where they
were sitting and sat down in an empty chair next to Ralston's.
"Hello," he said to each of them with a somber politeness
which seemed radically out of place in this bar — and then to
Ralston, "I'm Rudolf Talcott."

Ralston extended his hand, "I'm Jim Ralston."

"You must be really making it," Petersen said to the boy,
"He told us his name was W. H. Auden. He bought us a pitcher of beer though. Will you buy us another pitcher now we
know your real name?"

"I'm sorry," Ralston said. "I only buy people beer when my
name is W. H. Auden."

The boy sat sipping at the beer he had carried in with him.
He seemed neither amused nor annoyed at the interchange.
Petersen turned his attention back to him. "You got some
bread, Rue? You got enough bread to buy us a pitcher or a
glass?"

The boy half turned toward Petersen. "You scrounge everybody," he said. "You'd scrounge God if you could catch him."

Washington Jones laughed a long deep laugh, again disclosing his un-Negro teeth in the process. "That'd be really something wouldn't it, boy, to make old Papa Daddy pay for a beer. And John's just the man to do it. A real God-catcher." He paused and looked at Rue, "No bread, really? We ought to do something to pay back Mr. W. H. Ralston's kindness here."

"Don't bother about me," Ralston said. He rose abruptly and went to the lavatory and then to the bar to get another bottle of ale. When he returned he was disappointed to find that the conversation was exactly where he left it. Gregory was telling about a party which had evidently taken place in someone's kitchen at five o'clock on the previous morning. He, then each of the others in turn, summarized the events of what must have been, it seemed to Ralston, a very hectic and very dull party, a party which might, and Ralston suspected that it did, have its only justification in that its events could be talked about, be edited collectively into some kind of coherence, in a bar on the next afternoon.

"And so Sonia said, 'You're the kind that never really makes it, the kind who can't stand for there to be a great artist, the kind that killed Bird,' and then she threw a plate of scrambled eggs in his face."

"And most of them fell in Harry Winter's lap."

"I don't remember any of this. I must have been really out of it. David had given me five bennies and —"

"— then the stud that owned the pad came in with the landlord and —"

"— but there was still something left in the gallon winejug and —"

On and on they went in their relaxed Wonderland language, the boy next to Ralston neither more or less a part of the session (it more like a dull modern jazz record than ever, Ralston thought) than any of the rest of the combo. Clichés of excitement, secondhand enthusiasms, Ralston wondered why he felt so bitterly disappointed, so betrayed. Suddenly the boy turned to Ralston. "You hate things like that, don't you," he said.

"Not things like that, Rue," Ralston was immediately conscious of the ridiculousness of calling him by name. "Not things like that but the trying to put meaning into them afterwards."

"If you're going to talk you'll have to buy beer for us," Petersen said.

"Trying to make a mythology out of the dreadful scraps of your lives," Ralston continued as if he had heard nothing, conscious that this was probably his last chance to make a speech, "and making the scraps deliberately meaningless so that you'll have more fun picking them up afterwards."

"Don't put us down," Gregory said. "I hate it when people start putting people down. Like Curtis when he's drunk," he added, seemingly certain that the explanation would be as clear to Ralston as to everybody else.

"The gentleman that my friend Mr. Taxon is talking about," the tall Negro said from the distant superiority of his side of the table, "is a Flat Rock kiddie named Curtis Stein who always denounces our meaninglessness when he gets very lushed. Then he usually knocks a table over and passes out. I don't really see the similarity."

"I didn't mean to put him down or Curtis either —" Gregory began but the Negro stopped him in mid-sentence by raising one hand. "I'm sure you didn't," he said. "I was about to tell Mr. Ralston here that since he seems prepared to use our familiar names — and it is very kind of him to do so — that I am usually known as Judge and my friends here are known respectively as Greg and John the Scrounge. It is only proper to call us by our familiar names in any discussion of our faults."

"He was talking to me," Rue said and turned fully to face Ralston. "Do you know a better way of going about it?" he asked. Ralston knew that he was back to *their* conversation and that he was asking the question perfectly seriously for information rather as someone would ask about a special way of preparing bacon and eggs.

Three thoughts occurred to Ralston almost simultaneously — that he should not sound like a schoolteacher when he answered the question, that he really did not, or why was he there, have the answer to the question, and that, if he did not answer the question, a whole world of confusing possibility might be cut off from him. "I don't know," he said, and then the devil of his schoolteacher honesty made him add, "I'm not at all sure but I think that you take the normal fragments of life and try to make them meaningful. I think that anything besides that is cheating."

"Why?" The question in the boy's voice was still on the bacon and eggs level. So far Ralston was right.

"Because," and suddenly Ralston could not think of the reason; it was like forgetting what you are going to say in class, Ralston thought in the few seconds that it took him to stutter, "Because," and then the schoolteacher, the poet who, Ralston thought later, could almost literally not afford to be at a loss for words took over. "Because billions of people are being born, marrying, and dying in much the same way. Because you live or write about those things to try to make them clearer. Nothing else."

"Just better glasses to wear? Not a different room?"

"All the rooms are the same."

"Shit!" Anger, disappointment, and frustration were all in the boy's voice. Then his voice changed and it became the voice of a member of the modern jazz combo, of the Mad Tea Party. "May I look at this for a moment?" he asked, pointing to the copy of *Partisan Review*, which was still in front of Ralston on the table.

Before Ralston could say yes or even wonder at the change in his voice, the boy had taken up the thick magazine. He held it for a moment in his huge hands and then, like someone doing a trick with a telephone book at a party, tore the whole lengthwise and crosswise in two quick motions. It was so quick and so, it seemed at the time, natural a gesture that Ralston could first only think of the strength of the hands that were doing it.

Then anger came. Anger was always a delayed emotion with Ralston. He would often know intellectually that he would be angry, he should be angry, before he actually could be. For what seemed like five minutes but what was actually, he was sure, no more than five seconds, he surveyed the scene like some great prehistoric beast whose nervous system is too sluggish to convey to his brain the pain of a death wound his eye could already see. Then anger came. "Damn you," he said. "Damn all of you. Snotnosed little boys tearing up things you don't understand. When I come in next time I'll bring along some pretty books for you to burn and some paintings you can slash." He stood towering over them in the fullness of his anger.

Rue stood up too. "I —"

"Baby," Ralston shouted. "Playing on the floor with rattles and wine bottles."

Rue's face had turned white. Ralston could see it more clearly, in his anger, than at any time that afternoon. It was the face of a beautiful marionette, a haunted doll, staring whitely down at him from the distance between their heights. Then, with a gesture of his hands Ralston could not interpret, he walked, slowly, jerkily, out of the bar.

"You really shook him up," Washington Jones said. "The gentleman is really shook up."

"Excuse me," Ralston said, looking down at those remaining at the table from a great distance. "Excuse me." He picked up his glass and went over to the bar to finish his ale and his anger.

He not only finished that ale but had at least another as well. Later when he tried to figure out how long he had been there at the bar alone (and it became important to discover this in order to explain the conjuring trick that followed) Ralston could not tell if he had been there ten or forty minutes. His sense of time was usually connected to (or perhaps measured by) the changing pattern of his thoughts — and his thoughts had been meaningless, not incoherent but meaningless. He doubted that at any one minute during that time he could have told himself what he had been thinking about at the minute before.

Ten or forty minutes. And then he heard loud voices from the table behind him. "What you got there, Rue?" Petersen's and Jones'. "My God, he's got a fish in his hand. Look, a fish!"

He looked in the bar mirror and saw the boy coming toward him. His face was full of color now and he was carrying a fish in his right hand, Ralston saw as he came closer to the bar, a fairly large black fish. Ralston turned. Rue advanced toward him and put the fish down gently on the bar next to Ralston's ale glass. "Here," he said. "This is for you."

Ralston looked at the fish which was flapping a little on the bar, not quite dead. It looked even larger now it was out of Rue's hand. One horrible open eye stared up at him.

"Look," the boy said. "Look in his mouth."

In the fish's mouth tightly folded was a piece of paper. Ralston sat staring, not moving a muscle.

"Take it out. Read it. It's for you."

The fish's dying mouth opened and closed slightly making the paper move. Ralston, fascinated between horror and anger, extended his hand and gently removed it.

"It's for you," the boy repeated.

Ralston unfolded the wedge of paper. It was, he could see, two pages of poetry written in large childish handwriting. Without allowing himself to read so much as a word of what was written, he folded over the pages once and then methodically began to tear the paper to shreds.

"See," Ralston said, "I can tear paper too."

The boy watched the pieces of paper flutter down to the floor. He looked as if he were going to cry. "It was a poem," he said softly. "You bastard. Oh, you bastard." Almost as a single movement he grabbed the fish in his hand and ran out of the door. Ralston waited for a moment then stumbled out of the bar himself, in what he hoped was the other direction.

II

He had been in the hotel room two days when he received the phone call. "Hello," the voice said. "Is this Jim Ralston?"

"Yes."

"This is Madelaine Slingbot."

"Uh —"

"Madelaine Cross, you idiot. Arthur and I heard you were hiding out in town and obtained your phone number from a very secret spy. Did you murder somebody in Philadelphia?"

"Boston."

"Boston then. Do you realize that I haven't seen you in six years?"

"Eight."

"You always were depressingly accurate. Don't you really want to see us."

"Who?"

"Arthur and me, of course. You aren't really going to pretend that you don't know that I'm married to Arthur?"

"Certainly, Madelaine. I just got into town."

"Two days ago."

"That spy of yours must be very accurate."

"They always are. We trade them in for old copies of *Poetry Chicago* when they make a single mistake."

"Uh —"

"You sound just like you used to. Do you remember when you and Tom and I went to Hugh and Lydia's wedding reception wearing Halloween masks and Lydia's mother had hysterics?"

"That was over ten years ago."

"And the Green Ink Bandit?"

"What happened to Tom?"

"Haven't you heard that either? He got sick and had shock treatments and now he's teaching in a private high school in New Mexico."

"When did all this happen?"

"It must have been three years ago. It was a year after I married Arthur."

"You know I'm married too?"

"I know all about it. A nice New England social worker. My spies in Philadelphia tell me everything. But I can't keep talking now. I have to feed the children. There are four now, you know. One of Tom's that you never saw and two of Arthur's."

"Uh —"

"Yes. Well, Arthur and I want you to come over for dinner on Monday night. We're going to have a few people in afterwards that you'll want to meet. And I do want to talk to you alone for a little while, Jim, and sort of fill in."

The time was set and the address explained and she hung up. Ralston felt a little breathless. He had not wanted to see Slingbot and he had not remembered that Madelaine was married to him — not really remembered although he knew that he probably had — and he did not want to remember Madelaine Cross at all or the Berkeley that he (and now she) had left behind, and he wanted to stay in the hotel room and — what, to be left alone — no — to stay in the hotel room and drink brandy and then go out and walk up and down all the streets he remembered and then go back to his room and drink brandy and read a paperback mystery and then to go out to have dinner and then to walk up and down the streets he remembered —

But there were streets in Berkeley too. Dingy tree-lined college-town streets. Streets he remembered more intimately if with less love than any of the streets of San Francisco. And Madelaine and Tom had been his best friends (for a while almost his only friends) in those first amazing years after the war when youth was resumed after a two-year interruption (or a four-year interruption — it had been worse for other people) and it was not the same youth anymore and no one was in the place he had started from and the government was paying for things and he, to his vast surprise, was at the University of California instead of the small orangebelt college in southern California he had left for war from and there were names like Henry Miller and Paul Goodman and Kenneth Patchen and every day you were sure to hear a new name, glowing, as new names did then, with a kind of promise of the undiscovered, unimagined freedoms. And he had taken as many courses like

Sanskrit and History of Byzantium and Chinese Vase Painting
as the Veterans Administration would let him and had lived in
a small room on the top floor of a private house in the hills
above campus and the window in the shower (he had never
seen a window in a shower before or since) had given a complete view of the lights of San Francisco and Sausalito across
the Bay. And had worn his old khakis and his Eisenhower
jacket except that he finally ruined the Eisenhower jacket
trying to dye it red with Tintex. And most of his friends were
like him, back from the terrible boredom of the war (even
Henry, who had lost his arm at Cassino, felt boredom at it
rather than anger) young men in Eisenhower jackets wander-
ing around in a vast library which contained all the secrets
(and described all the pleasures) of the visible and invisible
worlds.

Tom and Madelaine had been important members of this
scene. Tom had been a conscientious objector during the war
— a fact that gave him a hero status in the Berkeley of 1946
and 1947 that someone with even so visible a sign of loss such
as Henry never could or would even expect to enjoy. Why this
should be was a mystery to everyone. Tom would agree and
even insist that the dullness of a conscientious objector camp
was equal to or perhaps greater than the dullness of, say,
Cassino and the decision necessary to reach either was equally
accidental and, in retrospect, equally meaningless. Yet the
attitude was there, accepted by everyone — Tom's position in
respect to Henry's was exactly that in equally 1946 and 1947
post-war France of a Maquis as compared to someone who had
merely lost an arm on the Maginot Line.

But if Tom was the hero, was in fact *the* hero in their
heroless universe, Madelaine was the spirit and the arrange-
ments, the voice and the auditorium, a kind of a combination
of a sibyl and a welcoming committee. It was her money (she
came from an old Berkeley family that had something to do
with engineering) that paid for the apartment (six dingy rooms
that opened on to each other and finally ended in a small
kitchen and an even smaller bath, dingy even when they had
painted some of the dingy walls with collective nonobjective
calcimine splashes during parties), the food (mostly things
that had to do with beans and eggplants but given freely, if

cooked badly, to anyone who came in between five and seven
in the evening), the coffee (probably the largest item of all in
the budget — there was always, even at four in the morning
when everyone was asleep, a pot of coffee boiling on the stove
and Ralston could not remember ever having drunk so much
coffee in his life — coffee at the time was not merely something you had with dinner, it was used to induce all the states
of tension and relaxation that liquor, marijuana, tranquilizers
and even vitamin pills were used for later), and the most
important contribution of all, the two hundred dollars needed
to pay an anarchist's cooperative in New Jersey to print the
first and only issue of a little magazine that Tom and she and
Ralston and Henry and so many other people collectively
edited.

At the time Ralston had thought that everyone who went
to the apartment had been in love with Madelaine. He knew
that he was, that Tom, being her husband and the hero she
was basically the reception committee for, must of course be,
and Henry, in his pedantic and embarrassed way, and the
other young men, back from the wars or the conscientious
objector camps or the aircraft factories, and even the very
occasional young woman (so very few of them) it was possible
to imagine that even they were caught up in the spirit of the
thing, that even they in some mysterious way were in love
with Madelaine. It was only later, when Ralston had left off
his Eisenhower jacket and his belief in the infinitude of libraries, that he saw (reconstructed rather, he was always recon-
structing through the past like someone following by radar an
object just after it had passed the outer range of his vision)
that Madelaine, while the center, was by no means the only
object of the erotic currents that ebbed and flowed around her,
that she had known little or nothing about the French poetry
she was always talking about (and that most of the others had
known this), that she had not bathed regularly, not out of
defiance of any convention but out of sheer laziness, that she
was not even unfaithful to Tom.

But for years for Ralston, long after he knew these things
very well, she was the image called up at any moment of his
disillusionment with a woman. When a girl would lie to him
cheaply and obviously he would remember that Madelaine had

lied to him exactly in that manner and he had never caught her at it until now, when a girl showed a stupid enthusiasm for a good poem it would suddenly occur to him that Madelaine's enthusiasm for his good poems had been exactly that kind of stupid enthusiasm, when a girl who did not mean to go to bed with him kissed him as if she meant to go to bed with him it would occur to him (even in the moment of that kiss) that Madelaine must have been a prick teaser. This too had passed in time (long after the memory of the Eisenhower jacket and the infinitude of libraries seemed quite as far away as the memory of the clothes and thoughts of farthest childhood) and he had now, actually, until the phone call forgotten that she existed, or that Berkeley existed, or that he ever had been twenty-one.

And now she was married to Slingbot. He would not think of all the clever practical changes that would have come over Madelaine now she was in the new position (or, worse yet, about her being married to Slingbot and remaining just as she had been). For he had always disliked the man — even in those days when Slingbot was a semimythological creature (surely a demigod if Tom was a hero) who had managed to avoid (by reason, Ralston supposed, of his age) not only the boredoms of the army and the aircraft factory, but also the equal but more heroic boredoms of the conscientious objector camp and the jail. Slingbot remained where he was and what he was, spiting the war, resplendent in his own San Francisco, having a splendid active time writing poetry and telling young men not to fight, the only man who had not been bored during the war.

This was all very amusing now and slightly ridiculous, but at the time Ralston had felt really guilty for disliking the man, had wondered if the reason for his dislike was not merely that Slingbot had never noticed his poetry, had never invited him to one of those large private dinner parties for visiting poets that Tom (but not Madelaine) got invited to, in short, because Slingbot had committed the sin of excluding him from the glittering inner world of poetry and anarchism. And maybe this was all. The man, he had not been completely excluded, he had met him at a few very large public after-dinner parties for visiting poets, had a certain charm and a great deal of wit.

Now that the tables were turned and Ralston was the one for whom the dinner party was given (it would not be large as Slingbot was on record as calling his present kind of poetry "academic square" poetry, but it would be adequate as Slingbot had included one of Ralston's earlier, very bad poems in an anthology of Post-War Verse he had edited two years ago), now that the tables were turned why not make of the both of them a tabula rasa and go into this thing (which he now couldn't get out of anyway) without prejudice? Besides, he had come to San Francisco to discover something and so far his only contact with poetry had been to tear it up in that bar the first afternoon and (he was not going to think about that now) and why shouldn't he go to Slingbot's dinner party?

But he was not going without preparation. Madelaine's phone call had been enough to frighten him into saying yes before he had decided to say yes. He wanted no more surprises, no more marriages he had forgotten about, no more important details he did not know. He needed filling in, and even if filling in meant calling and having dinner with one of the people of the past he did not want to see (and every one of them he could think of fell into that category at the moment) it would have to be done — and immediately.

Ralston thumbed through two phone books (San Francisco and East Bay) that his hotel provided. It was as he thought — no one that he at all wanted to see (assuming that he wanted to see anyone — he suspected that he had picked the names to be looked up first purposely from those least likely to be there) was listed. There was only (and he supposed he should have known this from the start) Henry — and his address was not three blocks from the address he used to have at the time Ralston left Berkeley, and his phone number (Ralston couldn't quite remember but was pretty certain) was the same. It would have to be dinner with Henry — Henry who had kept writing him letters for years after Ralston had left Berkeley for Columbia even though he almost never replied to them, who had been his last, almost unwelcome, link with California. He had enjoyed the letters, even waited for them, but, as he became less and less able even to think about writing a reply, had also resented them as invaders of his privacy like telephone calls to someone who no longer lived in the house, and

when, after a silence of three more years, he had received a
Christmas card from Henry addressed to his correct current
address in Boston, he was surprised to discover that his feelings were almost of pure annoyance.

And Henry was home. And would have dinner that very
evening. Or rather would cook dinner for Ralston. He was
delighted and, Ralston felt, not at all surprised to hear from
him. And this again was annoying. Ralston resented people
that had no trouble with the past, for whom there were no
discontinuations — only temporary absences, who could welcome home as if by appointment the Enoch Ardens of any year
of their lives. And I, he thought to himself as he waited in the
East Bay Terminal late that afternoon for an F train for
Berkeley — and I am so much not at home with my past that
not seeing a person for several weeks will make him disappear
from my life, will make him, his reality when he reappears,
almost as shocking as a ghost.

When the F train did arrive and Ralston seated himself in
the smoking section and watched through the window as the
train pulled itself from the ugly station into a brief and even
uglier view of the waterfront which lasted (Ralston could
remember and was not even impatient) exactly four minutes,
and then the bridge — the bridge that connected San Francisco of the specious present (Ralston could remember the phrase
from one of his philosophy lectures) with Berkeley of the
severed past. Everything was more beautiful than he had
remembered — the bay a particular shade of blue that reminded Ralston of all the other shades of blue he had seen the bay
become but not quite (it never was) the same. With all the
islands set in it (although one was a federal prison, another an
abandoned detention camp for immigrants, and the third, into
which the train would soon be passing, a naval base) it reminded one less of a bay than an inland sea, its changing blue
waters not connected to any ocean but shoring up its own
tides, giving passage to its own travelers, as separate and
distinct from the Pacific or from the rivers that emptied into it
as some small European kingdom might be from the greater
territories that surrounded it. He remembered that Tom had
once said, as they stood knee-deep in wild barley on one of the
higher Berkeley hills looking down from the east at the glitter-

ing length of it, how Tom had said, "What if we had been the first persons to discover this, to see all this bare without lights or anything. If we had just come over from the other side of the hills and seen this. Can you imagine?"

And Ralston had pointed to the bright skyline of San Francisco and said, "If it weren't for those buildings and the bridge I could imagine that San Francisco was an island and that the bay went on forever."

And Tom had put his arm around his shoulder and said, "I wish —"

And Henry, when they had gotten back from the hike and told him about the idea, had said, "I wish we could all of us colonize it."

And Madelaine had made it all into an amusing game by suggesting which parts each of them should colonize. He remembered that she insisted that he and Tom should colonize Angel Island, while she, she would pick exactly the spot on Telegraph Hill where Coit Tower would not then be, while Henry, Henry could have all of what would have been Oakland and the Alameda estuary.

And the bay was still there and Berkeley was still there and he would be looking at its tree-lined, half-suburban streets in a few minutes and he felt the same sense of exhilaration he had had two days before in the bar when he realized that he was in San Francisco on the edge of a new adventure. He felt this only for a moment. Then the bay disappeared as the train passed into the tunnel of Treasure Island and it occurred to him that a return to the past, however pleasing, was in no sense a renewal, that he was merely reciting the scores of old football games, that it might be that he was using the Slingbot party as an excuse to retreat into old memories because of what had happened in The Birdcage on Thursday, because the past was no threat to John J. Ralston and this specious present was, that this trip to Berkeley was less a sentimental journey than the frightened running of a child that had been given a bloody nose by an angel or a quarterback.

•   •   •

Henry's house was only two blocks from the first stop the
F train made in Berkeley. It was a very small house, called by
courtesy a garden cottage, although there was no garden,
which stood behind a three-story building. When Henry
opened the door Ralston was pleased to see that he had hardly
changed. He was taller than he had remembered, Ralston like
all short men never remembered quite how tall people were,
and his leonine face had still more of a sag to it (sag was not
the word, it was a tilt really, but since it tilted downward, sag
was the word that came to mind) and he still wore the left
sleeve of his coat cut so that the stump of his missing arm
seemed to be hidden but nonetheless showed in moments of
anger and friendship.

"Come in," Henry said. "I have lamb chops. Did I write you
that I've given up on Whitehead completely?"

Ralston came into the small living room. Fully one third of
it was filled with a small pipe organ of the type operated by
bellows. There were two couches — one for sleeping and one
for sitting. There was nothing else in the room, not even a
chair or an ashtray, but books. Three of the walls, including
the wall behind the sleeping couch, were lined to the ceiling
with shelves of them, put together simply with pine planks
resting on construction bricks, so unstable looking in their
height that Ralston suddenly had the mental picture of Henry
standing in the middle of an earthquake with thousands of
books and bricks and planks falling all around him, flailing at
the wreckage with one arm, being buried. There were books on
the floor already. Library books — there must have been
twenty of them and from five different libraries — all of them
marked in one place or another with a neat slip of paper.

"I've been rereading Kierkegaard and find him quite convincing. Sit down on the couch and I'll get you a glass of wine.
Have you read the new book on the excavations in the Vati-
can?" Henry stooped down and picked up a particularly large
book from the floor and placed it in Ralston's lap. "There was
an especially interesting shrine to Sol Invictus just below
where Peter was supposed to be buried." Then, as if he had
suddenly remembered that it had been more than just a few
weeks since he had seen Ralston, "You don't mind wine, do
you?"

"No," Ralston said, fingering the book that he had been handed so that Henry would go into the kitchen and relieve both of their nervousness. "No. I still like wine."

Henry left and came back with two different-sized water tumblers filled with wine. He placed them both on the floor. "How do you like my organ?" he asked.

"It looks beautiful," Ralston said.

"It only cost four hundred dollars. I'm giving music lessons, you know, and with my disability pension it was easy to save the money."

Henry had gone off to war two-handed with a vague talent and inclination for playing the piano. He had come back, one-handed, with a burning ambition to become a composer. Not, as he had explained to Ralston long ago, because he had lost his arm but rather because the loss of his arm kept music from being fun (no one with a vague inclination would try to play the piano one-handed) and made it into something annoying and difficult (the copying of a score alone) and thus exciting.

"Are you composing for the organ now?" Ralston asked.

"Yes, I'm composing church music. Two-handed Protestant church music. A couple of things have been played in, God help us, the First Baptist Church. I'm working now on what I call a Unitarian Mass, but no one seems to get the joke."

"Can you play some of it for me?"

"What? Certainly I could. I could transpose. But I promised myself — and I mean it, you know I mean it — that I wouldn't play you any music at all tonight, not even records."

Ralston realized (or remembered) how shrewd Henry really was. He had been dreading an evening of music with important questions forced in on his part only on occasions — and those occasions to be paid for by a particular request to have the next piece repeated. Nonetheless he felt he should make a protest, "I would love to hear —"

"Nonsense," Henry interrupted him. "You never did like music very much and then only under special conditions. Some day before you go back to Boston I'll play all my music for you and you can be very polite about it and even enjoy it. But not now. Tonight we'll just talk. What do you think about modern poetry?"

"Modern poetry? There isn't any modern poetry. And besides people don't read it." Ralston said this in the voice of an English professor they both had had who was famous for statements like this. His name had been Grimple and he had looked like W. C. Fields and generations of students, Ralston supposed, had debated whether or not these dicta were examples of conscious or unconscious wit.

"There are two kinds of people in the world — monists and dualists. And I hate dualists," Henry replied, and they began an exchange of Grimpleisms which led them pleasantly, easily back to the past that Ralston had left so long ago.

After the lamb chops had been cooked (very badly) and eaten with green peas and no potatoes or bread, Ralston began to question him about people they both had known. "Tom? Yes, I hear from Tom. He likes it in New Mexico. He's married to a nice half-Indian girl and the school can't fire him because he's the only man in the state that knows Latin. Shock treatments? Maddie was exaggerating. There never was any question of shock treatments. He just broke down like they do in old-fashioned novels — and he had to go to the loony bin to get them to put him together —

"Madelaine? Oh, she married Slingbot four years ago. Didn't I write you about that? Slingbot was giving a series of Thursday night lectures on anarchism at his house. You know — Poetry and Anarchism, Religion and Anarchism, Music and Anarchism — that sort of thing. Well, Mary, his first wife, could never get to any of the lectures because she had to work nights at the hospital. On the evening of his Ethics and Anarchism lecture (I hear it was wonderful) Mary got home at three in the morning, dead tired, and discovered that Slingbot wasn't there. She found a note from him in the kitchen saying that he was sorry but he loved Madelaine and that they, Madelaine and he, would be in Carmel for a week and would she please move out in that time and if a week wasn't a long enough time for moving that was all right but would she please let them know. Then he gave an address."

"What did Mary do?"

"She moved. She was a little bitter at the time but she's good friends with Arthur and Madelaine now."

"God!"

"I'm sure I wrote you that. Don't you remember? It was in
that letter where I talked about the relation of Spinoza to the
Zohar. I was wrong, of course. Everything I thought about
medieval Jewish thinking at the time was dead wrong, but —"
     "How did Tom take it?"
     "I told you. He broke down, went to pieces. His analyst (the
one he had at the hospital) discovered later that he never
really loved Madelaine, that he identified with her feminine
role and was really always jealous of the fact that she was a
woman. But, of course, he didn't know that at the time and he
was pretty broken up."
     "I'm invited over there for dinner Monday night. I don't
supposed she invited you for afterwards?"
     "Me? I don't go anywhere any more. I haven't been across
to San Francisco in a year and a half. Besides, Madelaine
doesn't really like people from Berkeley any more. She thinks
they're academic squares who lynch Negroes."
     "If you never go out you must find it hard to keep track of
people —" Ralston began, planning to use the sentence as an
opening gambit for obtaining information about other missing
friends. But Henry was too quick for him:
     "Nonsense," he said. "Sheer nonsense. I keep a closer track
of my friends than anyone I know. And all because I don't use
a telephone."
     "A telephone?"
     "A telephone. Of course. The secret is in not using a tele-
phone. I have to have one on account of my music lessons, but
I never call up friends. Never. I always write them letters —
even if they live as near as three blocks away from here."
     Ralston felt a pang of guilt. "What if they don't answer
your letters?" he asked with a fixed smile.
     "That's the diabolical part of it. No one can answer all the
letters — so they feel guilty. He wrote them all for me with
only one arm they say. So they finally sit down and write a
real letter that contains real news — more than I could get in
fifty conversations or a thousand phone calls."
     "And if they don't?"
     "If they don't, they come to visit me like you did. And tell
me everything because they feel even more guilty when they
face me. Come and look at this." He led Ralston into the

kitchen and opened a large cupboard in which pots would normally be kept. It was filled with what seemed to be hundreds of enormous manila envelopes. Henry took out two or three of the thickest of them. "See," he said, holding up one with a picture of an alarm clock (probably from a magazine advertisement) pasted on the cover, "Madelaine writes to me even though she's only ten miles away and dislikes me."

"Do you tell who it is just by what's pasted on the outside?"

"Sure," Henry said proudly. "If I forget the symbol it's a sign I've forgotten the person and then I never look in the envelope again. There are about twenty of them in there like that." He reached inside the cupboard again and brought out a much thinner envelope with a picture of a can-opener pasted to the cover. "Here's yours," he said.

"Why a can-opener?" Ralston said, a little fearful of the answer he would receive.

"I don't know. I just let my subconscious work. At the time I started this I believed in the subconscious, but now I'm not sure at all. I think it was Unamuno who said that the subconscious was mankind's attempt to give meaning to the accidental. This can-opener for example. It might be possible that I merely saw a picture of a can-opener and juxtaposed it to the first person I thought of — which happened quite by accident to be you — like Hume's refutation of cause and effect or Spinoza's thinking arrow —" He interrupted himself suddenly and reached with his one hand into the envelope. "Oh, you might be interested in this."

Ralston knew what it was going to be even before Henry brought it out, even before Henry mentioned it. It was a copy of *Pillars,* a copy of the first and only issue of the little magazine they all had edited so long ago in the past. He stared at the red cover with the green pillar on it (which showed up black due either to the limitations of the ink or the printing experience of the anarchist cooperative in New Jersey), and the lower-case letters of the title and the proud, optimistic *September 1947* below it. Ralston had not, of course, forgotten that it had existed, but he had, certainly, forgotten that it could still have existed except in the sheer act of remembering. He took it in his hands, wondering what to do with it. "Yes, I remember this," he said.

"Remember this?" Henry was indignant. "Of course you remember it. I still show it to everybody who comes over to visit me. It was a beautiful magazine. There has never been anything like it."

Ralston turned the pages mechanically. The two hundred copies (was it really two hundred?) that it had sold must all have vanished into bottom drawers or trunks or waste baskets, except for one or two still living anachronistic copies like Henry's which would be housed, fed, and worshipped by their owners like a totem or a Siamese cat. No one would ever do that for the magazines he published in now (he was charmed at the thought of someone keeping a copy of *Partisan Review* that way), but there must have been literally thousands of one-issue little magazines in the last fifteen years in America which were still being kept alive, still being fed readers by guardians like Henry — the one or two surviving copies still yowling hopelessly from somebody's kitchen. The thought depressed him. He had found his own poem in the magazine. "God, that was an awful poem," he said.

Henry looked worriedly over his shoulder at what he was reading. "Yours? It is not. It's a beautiful poem. A really beautiful poem. I like it much better than the rhymey stuff of yours you're writing for Eastern magazines these days. I really don't mean that," he added with a nervous smile. "I haven't seen many of your new poems and you know I don't know anything about poetry. But still I think this one's a beautiful poem."

"'Elegy for a Hunter'," Ralston read the title aloud. "I wonder why I called it an elegy? We seemed to call everything an elegy that was over fifteen lines long."

"The section about the dragon," Henry began. The poem had been long and divided into sections, each of which described an animal (a thinly disguised version of the poet himself) that someone was or had been hunting.

"I wasted more lines in that poem than in any poem I've ever written," Ralston interrupted. "'The dream of red gold lost upon the shore.' Could you tell me what in Christ's name I meant by that?"

"From what standpoint?" Henry asked. "I mean even you
didn't know you didn't know Jung at the time but from a
Jungian position the red gold —"

"Henry, shut up," Ralston said. He turned the pages past
his own poem to the forty-page short story of Madelaine's
which took up the last half of the magazine — it had been
about a migratory worker and a bird and had been titled
"Skies of the Wingless" — and then to the front and the three
antiwar poems of Tom's — they had been about the atom
bomb and conscription and the right of every individual to
moral and sexual freedom. And then the other poems by other
people who had helped put out this magazine. "Besides," he
said in apology, although Henry did not in the least mind
being told to shut up, "besides the best contribution was never
printed."

He was shocked as he said this to realize that what he said
was perfectly true. The article that Henry had written on the
similarity of Baroque church music to some kinds of modern
poetry, it had been fifteen pages long and Madelaine, at the
last moment, had decided not to include it, was the only thing
they had either printed or considered printing that Ralston
today (as an objective observer) would have the least interest
in reading.

"So you remember that article, do you?" Henry was
pleased. "I've revised it twice since then and it's over thirty
pages long now. I'll mail it to you at your hotel and you can
read it when you're not busy at — By the way, what are you
busy at?"

This was Ralston's cue and he took it. Henry seemed to
know a surprising amount about Anne ("I have one of her
articles from the *Psychiatric Journal* in your envelope," he told
Ralston. "She seems to be quite level-headed. One of that new
neo-non-Freudian school, isn't she?") and he was able to understand the explanation about the fourth quarter of the football
game, it seemed to Ralston, very well, although he was contin-
ually interrupting him during this part of the story to ask for
details of just what plays the quarterback was calling ("It's
important for me to understand the qualities of imagination
you admired in him, don't you see?"), the basic offensive for-
mations both teams were using (and he was off on a five-

minute discourse on how the current popularity of the Split T
formation reflected the basic insecurities of American culture
in a nervous world — "a spread offense, it's like an anti-mis-
sile-missile") and even the place in the stadium where Ralston
was sitting when he was watching it. It all had come through
to Henry, Ralston supposed, although he had several times
lost the point of his own story in the maze of imposed foot-
notes. "So you see, I've come here just for this summer to
discover if there isn't something I've been missing, something
that makes a poem important enough to take those chances
for."

"Slingbot's party doesn't sound like quite the answer for
you," Henry said, "although you'll meet some interesting types.
Do you know what that old swindler is doing now? He's holding sessions in group analysis."

"Not at parties?"

"No. It's quite serious. He finally read a book on psychology." Henry imitated Slingbot's mellifluous voice that sounded,
as Ralston remembered it, like a combination between Ida
Lupino and Mr. Pickwick: "Actually I've always been interested in psychology. I remember once in Vienna in 1933 when I
told Sigmund Freud (that was before the Stalinists took him
over) what Carl said to me about the role of the creative
imagination and Sigmund said, 'Arthur —'"

"He doesn't really say things like that."

"No," Henry admitted. "Although I wouldn't be too sure.
Slingbot's always parodying himself in order to encourage
others to parody him. It's his most effective form of free publicity."

"But he's actually running sessions of group analysis?"

"Not exactly group analysis. The groups are limited only to
poets." Henry assumed Slingbot's voice again, "This is not
therapy for the personality. All personalities are sick in our
society. This is therapy for the poems."

"Then it's just a glorified poetry class?"

"No. Of course, I've never been to one of them but I hear
that it's much more exciting than that. They talk about their
morbid personal problems just like you do in group analysis
and then bitch at each other just like you do at a poetry class
— only they have more ammunition."

"Does Slingbot unveil his soul too?"

"No. He's the leader. They're supposed to transfer to him. He just keeps things stirred up and occasionally makes comment on the poems. He charges five dollars a session if you're interested."

"Uh."

"It's not really so sordid. I have a theory that anything like that which is done as a game (and this is a bit like playing Post-office) is better than anything which is done seriously. Slingbot subconsciously realizes the creative force of nonsense. But you still haven't told me how you're going to go about looking for football players or angels or whatever they are."

"I don't know," Ralston said. "I guess I'm planning to let whatever it is seek me out. That doesn't sound much like fourth quarter stuff, does it?"

"You're sitting on the bench waiting for the coach to send you in," Henry said. "You can't run unless they give you the ball."

"I'm not sure they didn't give me the ball the first afternoon I was here —" Ralston began, but Henry was riding off on a wild pursuit of a definition of the nature of the creative act involving in rapid sequence Red Grange, Cocteau's Heurtebise, Easter Island, Plato, Wordsworth, King Asoka, and the Magna Mater. When the animal was cornered, or at least winded, Ralston was able to ask, "Have you ever been to The Birdcage?"

Henry, not in the least breathless from his adventure, showed that some of his thoughts at least had stayed behind with Ralston. "The Birdcage," he said. "That's where you went on the first day. And that's why you sounded so unconfident when I asked you where you were going to look around. You've been to The Birdcage and seen our Beat Generation."

"They're nobody's Beat Generation. They're just like the Bohemians in New York or Paris or Wichita Falls. But something did happen that upset me."

"I was only there once," Henry said, not really interrupting Ralston, for Ralston had paused between sentences. "Last year. On what they called Dada Night. I had been reading about the history of Dada in that wonderful Motherwell anthology. I'll admit freely that I merely visited the bar to confirm my prejudices. There just can't be an American Dada any more than there can be an English Dada or a Japanese Dada. Dada can't exist on islands." He paused in order to give Ralston time to ask why Dada could not exist on islands. When Ralston was silent, he reluctantly continued the main thread of his story. "It was terrible. Mad Comics stuff. Pictures of Mother with a knife through her heart, saxophones stuffed with eggplants, parodies. I started talking to a tall Negro who was wearing a suit put on backwards (I wonder how he ever got out of it) and told him what I thought of the whole performance. He told me, and I quote him literally, 'Daddy, this isn't just Dada, this is *cool* Dada.' Cool Dada!"

"I think I met the person you're talking about the other night," Ralston said.

"You couldn't have because I just invented him as an example. Anyway, I told him that it was impossible to draw a mustache on the Mona Lisa if you don't know where they keep the Mona Lisa, that Dada was the destruction of excess baggage and I didn't see the point of people who didn't have any baggage going around burning up imaginary bags."

"It sounds like a wonderful conversation."

"It would have been. Actually I didn't talk to anyone that night. They all looked as if they had read five books. People are so terribly sincere that have read five books."

"It's easier now that you can buy all five of the books in paperback."

"And five unbreakable long-playing records. And each person has a different set of the five important books bought in paperback and the five unbreakable long-playing records and they can exchange notes from them and it will be conversation. No, I didn't say a word."

Ralston knew, and Henry knew that Ralston knew, that his lack of conversation on that Dada Night, if, indeed, Henry had not invented that Dada Night as a kind of moral example, had nothing to do with his attitude toward the people present but stemmed from a curious kind of paralysis of the imagination that affected Henry whenever two or more people were, or seemed to be, listening. With a single person, even, say, a milkman, Henry's rhetoric (understood or not understood) could not be denied, could open (understood or not understood) a hole beneath one's feet. With a group of people (even the most understanding and educated) it merely (to change the metaphor) echoed. Ralston could imagine how a bar, and a bar like The Birdcage, would affect him.

"Now tell the story of your first afternoon in The Birdcage. I'll keep quiet. Honestly I will."

But what did Ralston want to tell him? That he had met a person that had torn up his copy of *Partisan Review* and given him a fish with a poem in its mouth and that Ralston had torn up the poem? Or that Ralston had met a number of strange people and that he felt that he had, in their language, goofed — not in relation to them but in relation to what he was presumed to be searching for? Or that he had discovered that bars could have plain unpainted glass windows and that he could have a sudden spasmodic recognition (the wrong word and so much the wrong word for Henry who would ask what it meant) of a person with whom he could have no possible relation or identity. Or that all this had, to use their words again, flipped him for two days afterwards, flipped him at the moment, quite as badly as he had been flipped at the time. "Just the same thing that happened to you," Ralston said. "Only the whole thing made me feel stiff and academic — and old, of course."

"Academic. Well, I'm not academic," Henry said. (They both knew that he had been protected from becoming a college professor by his inability to face crowds.) "What chances do you think *they* take?" His *they* by some magic included all the people that he knew that Ralston was thinking about but not mentioning.

"*They* won't be leaving for the East to become college professors," Ralston said. "Not even the worst of them."

"They couldn't if they wanted to. But suppose one of them was able to. Do you suppose he'd have the guts to come back afterwards like you did?"

"Or the naiveté."

"Fourth period quarterbacks are always naive. These people are cool and cool means staying in the same place you already are."

"They — ?"

"I mean the people that are younger than we are and are like we are and aren't. I mean the Beat Generation. I mean the Cool Generation."

When someone attacks something that I am afraid of or envy, Ralston thought, whether it is a poem or a person, I always feel pleased but I always think a little less for the moment of the person that has pleased me. Not quite think less but think of him in caricature, see Henry, while he tells me that cool people always stay in the same place, as Alice's White Knight on horseback with mousetraps and honeycombs and pipe-organs overbalancing his saddle-bags. Too full of invention to know despair, too ingenious to tear a *Partisan Review* or to bewilder or be bewildered by the gift of a fish. And yet what he said was true. What he stood for could not be dismissed as merely academic. "Henry," Ralston said, "would you do me a real favor?"

"You'd better name it first," Henry said. "I don't often do favors for people."

"Could you come to that bar with me some night? Maybe even tonight. I'd sort of like to see it through your eyes, to get the taste of it out of my mouth."

"What happened that afternoon?" Henry asked. "What happened that afternoon? You haven't told me yet."

And Ralston told him. Told him with all the oversimplifications that he knew he would use. For once Henry did not interrupt. When it was all over he asked, "Where did he get the fish from? You say the fish was still alive. Where do you suppose he got it?"

"Just barely," Ralston said. "Just barely alive. I don't know where he got it. He'd have had just about time to take a taxi down to the fishing pier at Aquatic Park and buy one from someone who had just caught it there. But I'm sure he didn't have enough money for a cab, and besides, why should he bother?"

"An intercepted forward pass," Henry said. "I'm not an exorcist. I can talk very well about magic but I'm not an exorcist. You'll have to deal with this thing by yourself."

"Oh, that's not the reason I want you to go to the bar with me. He wouldn't be there anyway. I'm not asking you to come

with me on account of that. I just want to have someone with
me that could —"

"No. I couldn't do anything. Besides I hate bars."

Henry remained firm and they talked about other things.
Ralston stayed for a half an hour longer and then rose and
walked to the door. Henry rose with him, the stump of his arm
showing briefly from his right sleeve. "Don't worry," he said.
"You'll have a fine summer. Come back and visit me. And if
anything like the fish happens to you again recite the Declara-
tion of Independence under your breath."

"Shall I give any message to Madelaine?" Ralston asked.

"Don't bother. I'll write her a letter."

III

The morning before Slingbot's party, Ralston had a dream. It was not a nice dream and, for that matter, the hotel bed was not a nice bed to dream in. He was in a large city on a coast (rather like Atlantic City) and was about to build a large apartment house out of sand. The beach from which he was to gather the sand was covered with beach umbrellas which were of every color that anyone, even in a dream, could possibly imagine and he could see the gray water behind the beach umbrellas slopping away at its own purposes.

The apartment house looked like a large birthday cake. This is the tower of Babel, he thought, this is really the tower of Babel, and he could remember wondering vaguely how elevators could run through sand.

He was on the top of the tower now (although workmen were hanging around trying to construct another top to it) and he was saying to somebody, "This reminds me of a poem. I shall have to write a poem." Then he saw a big whale coming out of the water and the tower fell (slowly as if sand were the proper means of construction) and he, having, he supposed, wrenched himself out of the dream and into another, was with Rue and Washington Jones on the beach picking seaweed. The beach was full of seaweed and they needed seaweed (confused somehow with driftwood) for starting a fire. "To build a fire," Rue said and Ralston woke up remembering very clearly that "To Build a Fire" was the title of a Jack London story about a man who froze to death.

Since he had planned to phone Anne that day (she wouldn't really worry but it would be a nice thing to call her) he almost immediately began remembering, began fixing his memory on the dream ("You're so superstitious, darling. You'd believe everything I told you. Besides, I love you for your conscious aggressions not your unconscious ones.") and he had no intention of telling the dream to Anne, but it was fun at eleven o'clock in the morning in a not very satisfactory hotel to analyze the dream as Anne might (but wouldn't) have analyzed it.

Since the tower (or apartment house that had become the tower) was too obvious a phallic symbol really to be phallic ("The language of dreams changes like the language of slang," Anne had once told him when he was expressing extreme disbelief at something of Freud's he had been reading. "Those early dreams that Freud analyzed are hard to believe in the same way it's hard to believe that anyone ever really said 'Twenty-three skidoo.' No one would dream of a penis being a snake nowadays. Not if they really meant it.") Since it was not phallic, it must symbolize his urge to discover for himself a new kind of poetry — the Tower of Babel (an obvious pun) — both a criticism of and an aspiration for the poetry that he had hoped he would discover here. And the whale that had destroyed the tower (but why was it originally an apartment house?) was obviously connected in some way with the fish that Rue had given him. But why the switch to the seaweed that was really driftwood and the fire — and why the sudden vision as he was waking up freezing? And why wasn't Henry, whose conversation had been so important, in this dream about poetic achievement, or Slingbot and Madelaine whose party he was soon to go to? Maybe it was all sexual. He was damned (and suspected a sly pun beneath the phrasing of that statement) if he knew. The dream analysis had reached a self-parodying stage. He would get up and make a long distance call to Anne at the clinic. He would tell her, within the limits of truth, that he was all right, that San Francisco was cooler in the summer than Boston, and that, if the dream showed nothing else, he missed her.

Which he did. Phone her and miss her more after than before the phone call. They were able to say nothing to each other within the limit of their three minutes and to extend the call beyond the minimum time of long distance rates would merely have emphasized this lack of anything to say. She did suggest, and this was the only thing he remembered afterwards of the conversation on either of their parts, that he move out of the hotel room and into a small apartment of some sort ("You don't have to tell them that you'll only be staying for a couple of months — and you'll save money and be more comfortable. Besides, you don't sound like you're really there yet.") The phone call did nothing to solve the mystery, if there really was one, of the dream or to restore (or, for that matter, shake further) his confidence in the role he was going to be forced to play in the dinner party that evening.

Madelaine and Arthur lived in a large flat high up in the Potrero Hill district of San Francisco. It seemed to Ralston, when he had finally climbed the seven wearying blocks from the bus stop to their house, a particular waste of a hill — the only hill in San Francisco from which, on this side of it at least, one could see absolutely nothing worth seeing.

Ralston rang the bell and climbed the stairs when the buzzer clicked him in. Standing in the entrance to the living room was a little girl of about seven or eight with long blond hair. She was wearing a red peasant blouse and a green skirt. She grinned at Ralston, showing in the process a set of ugly braces on her upper teeth. "Maddie's in the bathroom," she said. "She'll be out in a minute. And Arthur's gone to get rid of Pookie and Peter and pick up the Jap. Sit down on the couch and have a cigarette." As Ralston moved to the couch she had indicated, she ran out of the room laughing a childishly false laughter.

As Ralston sat on the couch wondering what on earth to do next, there was a sound of flushing from behind a door immediately to the right of him (who ever heard of a house where the bathroom opened directly off from the living room, Ralston thought); the door opened and Madelaine, looking exactly like the Madelaine he remembered, entered the room.

"Hello, Madelaine," he said, determined to have the first word. "You did say five, didn't you?"

She ran across the room and put her arms around him so that their faces almost but not quite barely touched. "Oh, Jim. It's so good to see you. Yes, I said five. I wanted to have a chance to talk with you before dinner. Arthur's gone out to leave Pookie (that's Arthur Junior but we call him Pookie) and Peter with the baby-sitter and to pick up the other guest. He's a nice Japanese gentleman named Mr. Hashiwara who is a Zen Buddhist monk somewhere in Indo-China. Arthur says he wears a yellow robe. We'll have over an hour to talk before they get back."

"Yes. The little girl told me," Ralston said.

"The little girl? Oh, Janie. Didn't you recognize Janie? I suppose you couldn't. She was only a baby when you left, wasn't she?"

"That was the baby? That was The Second Issue?" Ralston was illogically surprised. Most of the last year before he left Berkeley had been filled with the enormous figure of an unborn baby — called, even after the child had been born, proved to be female, and named Jane Elizabeth after both Madelaine's and Tom's respective mothers — The Second Issue, as a result of a remark that Henry had made the day that Madelaine announced to everyone's surprise, including Tom's, that she was completely sure that she was pregnant and that she intended to have the child. "That's just your way to get out of doing a second issue," Henry had said, meaning, Ralston supposed, that even pregnancy was not beyond Madelaine. And they had all referred to the bulge that kept growing larger and larger and more and more important until it became an actual baby in July as The Second Issue. And there had been, as Henry had predicted, no second issue to the magazine.

No father then (and no father now), Ralston had felt a vicarious sense of paternity toward the child before and after (at least, for the several months after the birth that he still remained in Berkeley). And so had all of them. Even though Madelaine had never been to bed with any of them but Tom, they all felt that any of them (because of the way they loved Madelaine) secretly could have been, secretly was, the father, that The Second Issue, that Janie, was as much the collective expression of all of them through Madelaine as the magazine was or the conversation at dinner.

"We don't call her The Second Issue now, of course," Madelaine said a bit sharply. "I'm glad you had a chance to talk to her. Isn't she an interesting child?"

"She seemed rather shy," Ralston said. "At the end at least." He suddenly realized that they were both still standing and moved toward the couch. "Isn't she used to strangers?"

Madelaine sat down beside him. "Of course, she's used to strangers. Everyone comes here. William Carlos Williams stayed here when he came to town. She wasn't a bit shy with him. She's not shy with anybody."

"Then why did she run away when I came in?"

"Oh, that. I see how you got the impression she was shy. Running away is a game with her. She runs away and hides. You never can tell where she's hiding. She's probably behind the couch right now." Ralston looked nervously over his shoulder but could see no little girl behind him. "It's all her age," Madelaine went on. "She's so much older than Pookie and Peter and the children in the neighborhood aren't really bright enough for her to play with. You get used to it after a while."

Ralston was not quite sure what the it was that Madelaine referred to, but he was resolved not to jump if someone popped out from behind a chair at him and shouted "Boo." It was time for a change of subject. "You look just the same as you did the last time I saw you," he said. "Just the same."

"Well, you certainly don't." Madelaine had not forgiven him for implying that Janie was not used to strangers. "Your hairline's beginning to recede and you're actually beginning to get fat. You always were so terribly thin in Berkeley, always looked like you were starving. Your wife must be a good cook."

"She doesn't have much time for cooking, I'm afraid. Neither of us do. I cook the meals as often as she does. After all, her work is more important than mine."

"I don't understand you at all. You used to think that nothing was more important than poetry."

"I meant my teaching," Ralston said.

"Oh, that! Why do you bother with it anyway? Doesn't your wife make enough money as a psychologist or whatever she is so that you can stay home and write?"

"That sometimes doesn't work out," Ralston said mildly.

Madelaine ignored or failed to understand the remark. "Arthur thinks a great deal of your earlier poetry," she said, "and he's disturbed about the effect that teaching in a university seems to be having on you. You're becoming one of those magazine poets."

"He publishes in magazines too."

"Yes. But they really don't want to print him. Not most of them anyway. They hate having to print poetry with real social content."

"My early poetry never had any social content."

"Well, I really don't know anything about poetry. Arthur always says that I have the mind of a prose writer. Would you like to look over the house? It's really beautiful."

Ralston rose with Madelaine. He did not bother to say that he had been to this flat several times before it contained a Madelaine and that it seemed, from the living room at least, remarkably unchanged. And she took him from room to room, describing the impedimenta of Slingbot's triumphs which were mostly in their familiar places — the inscribed photograph of Joyce ("When Arthur was in Switzerland"), the complete set of *transition* ("Jolas gave him all the missing early copies. Arthur almost become Jolas' secretary when he was a young man"), the framed newspaper photograph which showed Slingbot marching with some other people in a demonstration during the San Francisco General Strike ("Arthur was a terrible Communist during those days but so was everyone. It must have been thrilling."). Ralston was seeing the rooms through Madelaine's eyes and through Madelaine's possession that he had seen before through his own eyes and even before that that both he and Madelaine had seen through Tom's ecstatic descriptions of them. It was in only a few things like the bedrooms ("This is Pookie and Peter's room and this is where Janie sleeps") and the small television set ("We had to buy one as Arthur is often asked to read his poetry on the educational TV station, but we never turn it on otherwise. Don't you think they're hideous?") that Ralston could detect any change.

The dining room consisted mainly of one very long table which looked rather like an extended picnic bench. At the far end of it there was a serving window opening into an ancient pantry. (Madelaine now launched into a rambling and inaccurate version of the story that Ralston had heard Slingbot tell amusingly of how the house had been built by a retired New England sea captain who was afraid of water and how this was an authentic New England dining room and pantry.) Suddenly Ralston felt he could take no more. "I'm thirsty, Madelaine," he said. "Could I possibly have a drink?"

Madelaine looked uncertain for a moment and then looked up brightly and said, "Oh, yes. I think we can steal a little taste of the sherry before they get back," and Ralston knew that not even this had changed, that Slingbot was as frugal with his liquor as ever, and that there was probably only one fifth of sherry to last every purpose the whole evening.

"Let's go in and get it," Ralston said. He was not going to be stuck the whole evening with a small glass. With only one (or possibly two) fifths of sherry for an evening of guests, it was important not to be stuck with a small glass.

They went together into the pantry. From the kitchen on the other side of it he could hear the sounds of things boiling. He looked suspiciously at Madelaine wondering if, after all these years, dinner would still have something to do with eggplant. She had opened the cupboard and was extracting two small glasses. "No," he said. "I'll take the glass with the red rim on it. Don't you remember how I always like glasses with red rims?"

Madelaine did not remember, as indeed she could not, for he had just improvised the memory, but she meekly allowed him to take the large red-rimmed glass and to pour appropriate portions of the half-full bottle of sherry (there would be one and a half fifths) into her glass and into his.

They were standing next to the window of the pantry looking on into the half-lit dining room. Ralston felt much better. "Let's drink to something," he said.

"To the past, the present, and the future," Madelaine said softly — and they raised their glasses and drank.

Ralston swallowed half of his glass of sherry in one gulp. He went to the cupboard, took out the bottle and carefully filled the glass again to the top. Madelaine stared at him. He felt better now, much better. For the first time since he had arrived in San Francisco he was in control of a situation. He kept silent, forcing Madelaine to speak.

"Are you going to stay in San Francisco, Jim?" she asked finally.

"Why should I?"

"The Renaissance, I mean. The reawakening of poetry. Everybody's coming here. Hundreds of people. You've heard about it in the East."

"You must be having quite a time."

"I am. Oh, Jim, you don't know how thrilling it is. Everybody comes here. It's like having a party in the middle of an anthology."

"Not like Berkeley?"

"Sometimes I think that in our small way we helped to start it in Berkeley. All of us. With Arthur's help, of course. But it's so much bigger now. Almost international." She put down her small glass, empty, and Ralston poured some more sherry into it. "And now you've come back to us."

"Only for the summer," Ralston said. "I'm not an international poet."

"You've changed. You never used to say brittle things like that."

"You haven't."

"In a way I have." Madelaine's voice now sounded sad and distant. "I suppose you wonder why I married someone as old as Arthur?"

"Haven't you just been telling me?"

Madelaine looked closely at Ralston. "You've learned to make bitchy remarks to women," she said. "It must be your wife. Did she psychoanalyze you before or after your marriage?"

Then suddenly, almost inexplicably, she was in Ralston's arms and they were kissing. A long kiss. Several long kisses. "Oh, Jim," Madelaine said. They began to kiss again.

"I see you," a voice said. "Nyah, nyah. I see you."

Startled, they both turned. There in the serving window between the pantry and the dining room were the braces, the blond hair, and the rest of the face of Janie. Her hands were clutching the inner edge of the window and her head was partly into the pantry.

Madelaine slowly but firmly disengaged one of the hands and placed it into Ralston's: "Janie, you haven't met Mr. Ralston formally yet. Janie, this is Mr. Ralston."

•   •   •

Dinner was not a success. Slingbot, all 275 pounds of him, presided with dignity at the head of the table, trying in his most Pickwickian manner to combine shop-talk about New York publishers for Ralston ("I told Jimmie that if he published another dull novel by a North African at least he should make sure this time that the author wasn't a Stalinist. A

Trotskyite, yes. A Trotskyite North African novel would be amusing. But from what Paul tells me —") with what Ralston supposed was Zen Buddhist shoptalk for Mr. Hashiwara — who was indeed wearing a yellow robe ("All this nonsense in the *Lotus Sutra* about dharma. It's as bad as Puritanism. The freeing of the body from the wheel, certainly, but not all those circles, not putting rings on the absolute.")

Almost from the beginning things had begun to go badly. Madelaine had cooked four different dishes of vegetables in vaguely exotic fashion (spinach in tarragon vinegar, carrots fried with tomatoes, lima beans cooked with coconut, and puzzlingly good, cauliflower with mustard and cinnamon), a large pot of rice somewhat overcooked (which she spooned into Chinese bowls for each of them) and, to Ralston's delight as he did not much care for vegetables, sirloin tips.

Madelaine served the vegetables and the meat on each plate in turn (the plates were very ceramic, dating from a time in Slingbot's past in which he had had a kiln and a beard — Ralston thought they must be very hard to wash) and Mr. Hashiwara's plate she heaped with vegetables omitting the sirloin tips entirely.

They had begun to eat when Mr. Hashiwara looked slowly around at the other plates. "Excuse me, please," Mr. Hashiwara said. "Is it American custom that person on left get no meat?" He smiled and looked at each of them.

"Oh," Madelaine said. "I'm so sorry. I thought all Buddhists were vegetarians. I thought you couldn't take lives."

"No. In Zen we let things die. Things, people, everybody. Now if I throw the bowl of rice in your face, this is Zen." Mr. Hashiwara smiled again and hissed politely through his teeth.

"I'm sorry," Madelaine repeated. She looked around. There were no more sirloin tips left in the serving bowl.

"Westerners often get the wrong ideas about Buddhism, don't they, Seshumi?" Slingbot said. He turned to Ralston. "It's amazing how little Americans know about the thought of the East. I don't suppose there's one course in Oriental Buddhism at your university."

"Not even one course in Chinese or Japanese to read it with," Ralston said.

"That's the trouble with the academic mind in America," Slingbot went on. "No real education. They know all the New Criticism and don't even know the difference between Hinayana and Mahayana."

"Am I really not to get no meat?" Mr. Hashiwara asked plaintively.

Slingbot looked at the empty dish. "I'm sorry, Seshumi. It seems to have been all served. Madelaine could go out into the kitchen and fry you some bacon if you'd like. It's interesting," he said, turning to Ralston again. "Why do you suppose that English is the only language in the world that doesn't have a negative intensive?"

Janie had been sitting at the table all the while, the model of a silent eight year old, hardly touching her food. Madelaine, either to create a diversion or as an oblique slap at Mr. Hashiwara, said, "Janie dear, eat your vegetables."

"I can't," Janie said in a very small voice. "I feel sick." She patted her stomach. "I feel all oozy here."

Slingbot, momentarily disconcerted, led the attack on the other flank. "I suppose, Jim, you haven't had a chance to meet any of the new poets in San Francisco yet?"

"No," Ralston said. "I'm looking forward to. From their poems they sound like they've led very interesting lives."

"It's the difference between your generation and theirs. The war disturbed your lives and you've had to hide in universities and literary criticism. They don't have to hide in anything. They've never known anything that wasn't disturbance."

"The war disturb us very much in Japan too," Mr. Hashiwara said smiling at both of them. "Hiroshima."

"That was a crime, of course," Slingbot said. "But the crimes of peace are even worse than the crimes of war. You can put a hundred and fifty million people in a Buchenwald without any of them knowing it."

"I haven't really seen anybody," Ralston said. Madelaine came in with the coffee and, with a wink to Ralston, the remains of the first bottle of sherry. Slingbot stared at it. Ralston quickly filled his glass and continued. "I have been to one place you mentioned in your articles on the Renaissance — a bar called The Birdcage."

"Ah! And what did you think about it?"

"It was confusing. Not many of the people in it seemed to be poets."

"Not many people in little magazines seem to be poets either," Slingbot said acidly. "But I know what you mean. So many tourists have been coming there since I wrote my articles."

"They seemed more like habitués to me —" Ralston began, but Mr. Hashiwara, who had been sucking noisily on the last piece of cauliflower, interrupted him to ask, "This birdcage you speak of, it is in a bar?"

"No, Seshumi," Slingbot said. "The bar is called The Birdcage. It is a fanciful title like the names of bars in Paris."

"I am sorry. I have never been to Paris." Mr. Hashiwara smiled again.

"It is a place where poets and painters come to drink," Madelaine said joining the game, "and people who come to drink with poets and painters."

"And this drinking is of vital importance to your Renaissance?"

"It's hard to explain, Seshumi," Slingbot said, staring significantly at Ralston's now half-empty sherry glass. "In our civilization poetry and painting aren't integrated to the rest of the culture as they are in yours. The artist is an outcast. He is supposed to live on nothing and be a bit crazy — rather like your monks. People regard them as amusing and a little holy — both at the same time."

"We look on all human beings as that, all creatures," Mr. Hashiwara said.

"What Arthur means is that The Birdcage is rather like a monastery," Madelaine said. "The artists gather there and people come from miles around to laugh at them and get wisdom from them."

"At our monastery," Mr. Hashiwara warmed to his subject, "we hit visitors over the head with beanbags. That is, if they are truly seeking wisdom."

Ralston finished the rest of his sherry and poured another. There was only an inch left in the bottle. "You haven't explained to Mr. Hashiwara why all this is connected with drinking," he said.

"That's simple." Slingbot's voice was enthusiastic now, as if he found the theme for a new article. "Since politics died in the 1930s, drinking has been the only excuse for intelligent people to gather together in any heterogeneous group. It's dangerous to the police state to allow groups to assemble freely — but they still let them assemble to drink. It isn't very dangerous and besides the liquor lobby is too strong for them to stop it."

As often happened when he read Slingbot's prose, Ralston wasn't sure that he could identify all the themes. "The Birdcage certainly didn't seem much of a danger to the state," he said mildly. "With the exception of one beanbag thrown at me as I was leaving, I saw nothing but the same professional Bohemians that I used to see in the New York bars."

"There are people like that anywhere," Slingbot said. He turned to Mr. Hashiwara. "You must have people like that in your monastery. Professional monks. People who want nothing but the warmth and relative comfort that the monastery can give them."

"In Zen we are all professional monks," Mr. Hashiwara said.

Madelaine came around the table and refilled Ralston's coffee cup. He ignored it and poured the last inch of sherry into his glass. "Nevertheless," he said, turning to Slingbot and wondering whether to call him Arthur or Mr. Slingbot and calling him neither. "Nevertheless, they all look alike to me."

"Dylan said that too, but he meant something different by it." Slingbot had finally decided, Ralston thought, that only an anecdote, a famous Slingbot anecdote, would save everything now. "Dylan said that when I brought him into The Birdcage when he was out here the year before he died. That was the year The Birdcage first opened. We walked in the door with an old Negro prostitute we had picked up on Fillmore Street — she was a wonderful woman, she'd been part of the jazz scene in New Orleans when she was a girl — and Dylan was very drunk and had just tried to climb the lamppost at the corner of Union and Grant. I was trying to sober him up because he had to give a poetry reading for the squares at the University that evening —"

"Excuse me please," Mr. Hashiwara interrupted. "What is a square?"

Slingbot thought a moment for a translation. "It's hard to put it so that someone from your civilization would understand. A square is a person who is not enlightened."

"Ah!" Mr. Hashiwara said.

"So," Slingbot continued, "as we were walking through the door a big burly Texan got up from his table and —"

Ralston was never to hear the end of that story. At that moment Janie, who had become paler and quieter as the conversation progressed, jumped up from the table with her hand over her mouth and ran through the living room to the bathroom. In the distance sounds of retching could be heard.

Slingbot raised his immense bulk from the chair in a surprisingly agile way. "Excuse me, excuse us," he said. "We'll have to see what's the matter." Then he almost ran out of the room followed at a more hesitant distance by Madelaine.

It all went to show something about people, Ralston thought. He had never imagined that Slingbot would interrupt an anecdote, a famous Slingbot anecdote, for a child, especially a child that was not really his. But there it was. He looked over at the Japanese who looked back at him. "Do you suppose the meat was infectious?" Mr. Hashiwara asked.

"What?"

"The meat. The meat I did not eat. If you observe her plate you notice that she eat none of her vegetables only her meat. It is perhaps ptomaine," he added with satisfaction.

In a few minutes Slingbot came back carrying a piece of paper in his hand. "I wonder if you could do us a big favor," he said to Ralston. "Janie has a nervous stomach — it's a chronic thing — and we've run out of medicine. Madelaine doesn't want to leave Janie and I'll have to be taking care of the guests who'll be starting to come. Would you take my car and drive down and get this prescription filled?"

"I'd rather not trust myself with your car unless there's a tremendous hurry," Ralston said.

"Oh, no real hurry at all. I was just trying to save your having to climb back up the hill. The nearest drugstore is down at the bottom of the street you came up and then one block to the right."

"Well —"

"Don't worry," Slingbot said and he seemed to have a different, a more human voice now. "Janie often has these attacks. They're just bids for attention. You know she hides behind things and jumps out at people too. There's a bit of the actress in her like there is in Madelaine. But when she gets herself sick she really is sick. The stuff you're getting will just quiet her down. She's a nice little girl," he added. "Very much like I was when I was a little boy."

"Then there will be no party?" Mr. Hashiwara asked gloomily.

"Of course there will be a party. You answer the door, Seshumi, when Madelaine and I are in the bedroom with Janie and Ralston is out for medicine. It will be very impressive."

But the drugstore at the next corner at the bottom of the hill was not open. And he walked almost fifteen minutes down the street before he found one that was. After he had bought the medicine (a white liquid in a green bottle — some sort of bismuth preparation, he supposed), he wondered if he should call the house to explain why he would be so late getting back to it. Madelaine will think that I've stopped in a bar on the way, he thought. Dylan Thomas would have stopped in a bar on the way. I am not, thank God, Dylan Thomas.

But the train of thought continued as he walked back along the boulevard. He was too trustworthy, too (the word people really meant when they said trustworthy) predictable. If Dylan Thomas, sent out into the night on such an errand, had vanished for three days with the bottle of bismuth, Slingbot, when he appeared at the end of three days on his doorstep, would not have batted an eye. He passed a bar wistfully. It's too late now, he thought, I thought about it. Dylan Thomas would never have thought about it.

But there was a liquor store on the corner where he turned up the hill and as a compromise he bought a half pint of bourbon and put it in his coat pocket. It would be useful, he decided. He could, at the worst, when the second bottle of sherry was running out, take it into the bathroom with him — but it was a compromise, like his kissing of Madelaine had been a compromise, not what Dylan Thomas (he disliked the poetry but the figure was convenient as a symbol) definitely not what Dylan Thomas would do.

As he walked up the hill back to what he supposed would now be a party, Ralston did feel better. He was superior to these people (even to Mr. Hashiwara who was playing, after all, only a Japanese version of Ralston's own clown) in a way he was not superior to Henry or even Anne, in a way he could not feel himself superior to Rue. In this particular jungle he was a sniper (even when kissing Madelaine, even when buying the half pint of whiskey) while in Henry's or Anne's or Rue's world (jungle was certainly a melodramatic way to talk about Slingbot's world but it suggested its opposite) while in their world he was on the wrong side of a zoo.

The door was opened by someone Ralston did not know at all and the house was now full of people. Slingbot came up to him through the crowd. "I'm sorry you've had this trip for nothing," he said. "Janie is a little more sick than we thought she was. She's running a 102 temperature. We're going to take her to the hospital — just as a precaution."

"Can I help in any way?" Ralston asked. He felt indirectly upstaged by the whole event. This was to have been his night. He could compete with Mr. Hashiwara but not, definitely not, with a sick child.

"Well, if you could sort of take over the party while we're gone. I've already introduced Seshumi to everybody, but he's a little unreliable. We won't be gone long. I'm sure that there's nothing wrong with Janie but nerves, but we have to make sure."

The last thing old half-pint-of-whiskey Dylan Thomas Ralston wanted was to be more reliable than a Zen Buddhist while his host and hostess went out on a mission of mercy for a sick child. "I'll introduce you to them now, and then we have to go," Slingbot continued. He boomed his reedy voice (rather like a firecracker exploding in an oboe, Ralston thought), "Quiet! Quiet!" and in a minute there was actually quiet. He turned to the crowd (there were only ten or twelve people, but in the room and his public voice addressing them it seemed like an enormous crowd), "As you know, Madelaine and I will have to leave you for a few minutes. Let me introduce our other guest, Jim Ralston (he calls himself J. J. Ralston when he publishes in the square quarterlies), Jim Ralston, one of the few San Francisco poets to go East without completely losing his balls or his soul.

"When I first met Jim over ten years ago he was just a punk kid writing sonnets or something." He turned in studied informality to Ralston, "It was sonnets, wasn't it, Jim?" Ralston, who had not written in any conventional verse form until long after he left California, merely glared speechlessly at him.

"The San Francisco Renaissance has been going on for a long time," Slingbot continued, and Ralston could have sworn that he had not noticed the glare. "Jim Ralston is an example of a man who left it in its first stages but not before his poetry had obtained its drive and impetus from it, and now, after many years, he has returned to revisit us," the *us* had a modest royal sound to it, "and perhaps even to renew, to rehear his poetry through us. As I say, Madelaine and I have to be gone for a few minutes, but I hope all of you will introduce yourselves to Jim Ralston and afterwards, if he's feeling up to it, he may read you some of his poetry." Slingbot stopped formally and then said in a loud stage whisper to Ralston, "Your book's on the second shelf of the third bookcase. Most of them are university professors and crap like that so don't overextend yourself. We'll be back as soon as we can." He winked (a very unconvincing wink) and departed leaving Ralston (not merely the new Dylan Thomas Ralston but any possible kind of Ralston) hopelessly trapped.

In the process of leaving, Slingbot had maneuvered Ralston into his own chair, a big red-leather armchair that directly faced the rest of the living room. He sat there now, sullen, knowing full well what was in store for him. The first person to come up to greet him would be some particularly fatuous English instructor (or, worse, a graduate student) who really had read and liked Ralston's poetry and who would tell him this at great length, complimenting him, at great length, on his conservatism and discipline. All the others in the room would watch this interchange with knowing smiles — and they would be right because they *had* known that this idiot, whatever-his-name, would be the only person in the room who would have read and liked Ralston's poetry. And then a married couple both poets (he bearded, she in long braided hair)

who would live in some place like Sausalito would invite him
to dinner. And then two or three miscellaneous people who
hadn't read his poetry but knew they would dislike it (and
they would) would join the group and try to bait him about the
stuffiness of Eastern poetry. And then — It was too much. He
was trapped, he was trapped like an animal with a cord
around its legs that any escaping movement merely tightened,
like (and his images grew wilder as he waited for the inevitable English instructor to approach his chair) like a quarterback who was back to pass and the opposing line had broken
through red-dogging him and there is no receiver free to catch
the ball and if he goes backwards they would get him anyway
for a greater loss and there was no way of getting rid of the
ball — Ralston suddenly rose and went directly over to the
chair where Mr. Hashiwara was sitting with his arms folded
and a polite smile on his face. Ralston cleared his throat
loudly (a trick he had learned to perfection in the classroom)
and the room was silent. "I am sure Arthur has already introduced Mr. Hashiwara to you," he said, throwing the ball to the
only man on his side that was still in the backfield. "He was
telling us some fascinating things about Zen Buddhism during
dinner. You'll be seeing me around all summer but you'll
probably never have a chance to hear him again. Mr. Hashiwara, won't you tell them some of the fascinating things you
were telling us at dinner?"

   "I was only asking about meat at dinner," Mr. Hashiwara
said, either bewildered or pretending bewilderment. Ralston by
this time had already moved himself to the farthest end of the
living room (a safe distance from the damnation of the red-
leather chair) and was in the process of sitting on the floor. He
did not allow the voice to stop his movement but said (a little
less loudly for he was now a private person) "I mean about the
students and the beanbags, how you instruct people in your
monastery."

   The yellow-robed Japanese made a gesture of surrender.
"Mr. Ralston, I think, wishes to hand me a hot chestnut from
the fire," he said. "You would all very much rather hear his so
interesting poetry. But this does not matter. I will talk to you.
I have come all the way from Asia to talk to people. First I
must answer the question several of your people were kind

enough to ask. Why do I wear this robe." He paused and beamed at his audience. "I wear this yellow robe to fool Westerners. Now I tell a Zen Buddhist joke to fool Westerners. It is a very funny story about a man who commits incest with his daughter."

Mr. Hashiwara paused and beamed again as if he expected his listeners to applaud. There was instead a series of rustlings and slightly nervous laughter.

"There was a man in Benares," Mr. Hashiwara began, "who had a very beautiful daughter. One evening in July — it is very hot in Benares in July even in the evening — this man came upon his daughter laying naked in a hammock and he was overcome with her beauty and he raped her. He was torn apart with remorse, could not eat or sleep — even though she told no one about what he had done to her, did not even mention it to himself. After a few days of this bitter remorse everyone was noticing that there was something wrong about him, his wife, his business acquaintances, his neighbors. He was as pale as what we would call a fish ghost and his hair was falling out and he decided that the only thing to do was to look for a holy man and tell him what he had done and ask him what there was to do to make him good after such a crime.

"So he went to the temple of Shiva where he worshipped and asked for the chief priest and because the man was a rich merchant he was allowed to come near the inner temple and from a respectable distance to tell the chief priest his story.

"The chief priest was a very holy looking man with a long white beard and he listened to the merchant's story very intently. When the merchant had ceased talking the holy man fell silent for a very long time — in fact he closed his eyes and looked almost as if he were asleep." Mr. Hashiwara, disconcertingly, closed his eyes and made noises as if he were snoring. Several members of the party (or at least those that Ralston felt would best have fitted the parts that Ralston's imagination had assigned a few moments before) made small sounds of nervous laughter, but Ralston recognized a fellow professional and remained silent.

Suddenly from Mr. Hashiwara came the voice of the merchant, "'Honorable priest, please tell me how I can purge myself of this monstrous sin so displeasing to the gods. I will cut off my penis if they will it.'

"'My son,'" and Mr. Hashiwara was now a weary priest, "'It is indeed a monstrous sin. One that will be punished not only in life but after life is over. To cut off your penis would be nothing. It would be like destroying a knife which you had used to cut somebody's throat or burning a pocketbook from which you had refused to give alms.'

"'But what can I do? I cannot bear the burden.' The chief priest seemed to be asleep again." Mr. Hashiwara again resumed his insanely convincing snoring for a full minute. Then as before he took the merchant's voice, "Please help me. I will do anything.'

"'My son, you will give all your wealth and all your possessions to the temple. We will use them for sacrifices to Shiva and Vishnu. In this way we will cut at the root of your desire for things and your guilt will be forgiven.'

"And the merchant gave all his possessions to the temple and watched every day for two weeks while the priests sacrificed sheep with golden beads around their necks and monkeys with their eyes burned out with pearls in place of their eyeballs and dogs with diamonds sewn into their penises to the gods Shiva and Vishnu.

"When the ceremonies were finally over he felt like a new man. He was purged of all the guilt of having raped his daughter; he ate a large dinner and drank several glasses of mango wine and then went home, bankrupt but guiltless, to resume his life.

"But his wife was not there," Mr. Hashiwara in some Oriental attempt at climax had now assumed Slingbot's voice. "She had left him because he was bankrupt. He had come back to an empty home — except for his daughter who was lying in the hammock, still naked."

"Ha, ha," said a tall pasty-faced man in the audience whom Ralston had already identified as the English instructor who would be the first to talk to him and would really have liked his poetry. "That was a very illuminating story."

"It is not over," Mr. Hashiwara said coldly. "It has barely started yet. The sympathy that his daughter offers the unfortunate merchant, as some of you have already anticipated, is too great. He is overcome with emotion. In a moment he rapes his daughter again.

"Now he is really sorry. He goes out of the empty house sobbing. He says to himself I have given all my possessions and all the furniture of my house and even my wife to Vishnu and Shiva to be made into sacrifices to ask for forgiveness for committing incest with my daughter and now I spoil it all by committing incest again. He tears his hair and rushes into the streets."

Mr. Hashiwara paused again. He had his audience — even, in spite of the fact that he was the one that had thrown the pass, his quarterback Ralston who, hoping that the story was not too long, marveled nonetheless at the indirectness of the East.

"The streets of Benares are filled with holy men. The merchant sees one of them — a man who looks even holier and has even a larger white beard than the chief priest at the temple of Shiva. He is lighting pine branches with a torch and throwing them on a huge bonfire which is burning behind him although it is summer still in Benares and the day is very hot. This may be the very holy man who can help me, the merchant thinks to himself, so he lies prostrate down on the dirt of the road and says, 'Father, I seek forgiveness for monstrous sins.'

"The holy man says nothing and merely lights another pine branch." Mr. Hashiwara at this point took a kitchen match from his pocket and watched it burn to the very end. "'Please, father, I have committed incest with my daughter and been forgiven by giving all my possessions to Shiva and Vishnu and then, after I had been forgiven, I committed incest with her again. Tell me what I must do to obtain forgiveness.'" Mr. Hashiwara lit another kitchen match and remained silent while it burned. "'Please, father, what am I to do? Shall I cut my throat?'

"The holy man finally spoke. 'Your problem is that you are cold in the heart. Killing yourself would just make your heart colder.'

"'Then what shall I do?'

"'You will walk through fire,' the holy man said. 'You committed your great sins because your heart was cold.'

"The merchant was terribly frightened at the thought of walking through the holy man's bonfire, but he was even more frightened at the consequences of his sins. Following the holy man's directions, he stripped and rubbed his body over with a yellow salve the fire worshipper had given him and then stepped cautiously into the bonfire." Mr. Hashiwara lit another match and watched it burn. His audience shuffled impatiently.

"When he came through the other side of the bonfire," Mr. Hashiwara said finally, "he was burned but not terribly burned. The salve or his good intentions had protected him. In a few hours he was able to crawl home on his hands and knees. But even though he was in great pain throughout the journey he was in great pleasure — his cold heart had finally melted, he was forgiven all his monstrous sins.

"When he crawled through the door his daughter screamed. She insisted on carrying him to his bed and rubbing his blistered flesh with the salve that he carried with him. But as she rubbed his body he began to feel desire rising in his genitals. Before he knew it he had committed incest with his daughter again."

Mr. Hashiwara was silent, but none of the audience was to be caught by his silence again. Several shifted positions or coughed, but no one broke the silence. Ralston felt as if he had thrown the football to a halfback who had then done an Indian rope trick and disappeared into the sky with it.

Mr. Hashiwara began again as suddenly as he had left off. "The merchant lapsed into unconsciousness soon after he had raped his daughter for the third time — whether from his injuries or from overwhelming guilt I do not know. He spent six weeks in bed delirious and with raging fever. His daughter nursed him tenderly all the while. When he finally regained consciousness he could not bear to speak. When his daughter or anyone else came in to talk to him he merely turned his head to the wall. But one day his daughter came in with some news, news that penetrated the abyss of his blank despair. 'There is a new holy man in town, father.'" Mr. Hashiwara's voice now rose to a falsetto. "'He is a very strange and wonderful holy man. He has set cages of animals all around the marketplace and feeds people to them.'

"The merchant said the first word he had uttered in a month. 'Why?' he asked his daughter.

"'Something about curing them of their sins,' she said. 'He is a very holy man.'

"The merchant got out of his bed with a tired, agonized look on his face. He put on the only pair of clothes he now owned even though they had been badly stained by the yellow ointment, and he walked very slowly and very sadly to the marketplace.

"It was true. There were four cages set in the middle of the marketplace and each of them had a different animal inside it. In front of the cages stood a holy man with an even longer white beard than the other two had worn. Wearily the merchant began to prostrate himself on the ground and to tell his melancholy story, but the holy man stopped him with a gesture. 'Don't bother,' he said. 'I know all about you and what you have done. You have raped your daughter three times and now you have come to me to discover forgiveness.'

"The merchant nodded glumly.

"'Look at these cages,' the holy man said. 'Each of them contains an animal. Whoever seeks forgiveness must fight with the animal that he has inside him. Look closely at these cages and pick the animal that you wish to fight with.'

"The merchant looked closely at the cages. 'In the first cage is a fox,' the holy man said. 'In the second cage is a wolf. In the third cage is a crocodile. And in the last cage is a sick tiger. Which animal will you fight with?'

"The merchant considered for a moment. 'I have a sick tiger inside me,' he finally said. 'I will fight with the sick tiger.'

"A crowd had gathered by this time. They stood close by to watch the excitement. 'It will have to be a fight to death,' the holy man said. 'You will have to kill the sick tiger with your bare hands.'

"The merchant did not say a word. He merely stripped off his clothes and entered the cage.

"The fight between the sick tiger and the merchant was bloody and awkward. It lasted a very long time and most of the crowd had left before it was over. But at the end the sick tiger was dead and the merchant was victorious — although his face and body were horribly clawed and one arm had been torn away.

"The holy man was a healer as well as a keeper of animals and he tended to the merchant's wounds so well in his tent that in a few days the merchant was able to leave completely healed — although his face and body were of course now covered with scars and he had lost an arm and part of his nose and one ear was missing. 'Go now in peace,' the holy man told him as he left. 'You have killed the sick tiger in your body. You will never seek forgiveness again.'

"The unfortunate merchant felt a sense of elation that he had never felt when he had been forgiven before. He had killed the sick tiger in his body. He hurried home and his daughter met him in the doorway and screamed." Mr. Hashiwara stopped for thirty seconds and then screamed a piercing feminine scream. Then, in his own voice he went on, "But the merchant realized that fight with the sick tiger had so changed his appearance that his daughter might not have been able to recognize him. 'Do not worry, daughter,' he said. 'It is I, your father. I have just come from the holy man with the animals and he has made it possible for me to earn forgiveness by my own hands for the sins I have committed. We are poor now and I will never be able to earn money again, but I will beg in the marketplace and you will live with me in this home safe now from the ravenings of my lust.'

"The girl began to laugh. 'You old fool,' she said. 'The only reason I didn't leave you when you gave away all your money and your possessions was because you were still beautiful even if you were my father. Now you are mutilated and scarred and ugly. I am leaving you at this very moment and I will never come back.' As she started for the door he grabbed at her to keep her from leaving and in his rage and anger he raped her again."

Several new people had come into the room while Mr. Hashiwara was talking. He smiled at them now and said, "I am telling a funny story about a man who committed incest with his daughter. It is almost over now. Then I will tell it a second time if you wish.

"The merchant was not distraught this time. He was angry — angry at his daughter, angry at the holy man, angry at his own foolishness in believing in their cures. He walked up and down the streets of Benares muttering to himself. He spent three days doing this and at the end of the third day he decided to leave Benares forever. He wrapped his feet with rags and went out of the west gate carrying nothing but the soiled clothes on his back.

"He walked for days and days, still muttering to himself and still angry at everything in the universe. The stump of his arm was beginning to pain him and his legs ached from the walking and children would shout at him as he passed by. Finally he took a side road which seemed to lead away from all the towns and towards the mountains. He walked on it for two days and saw nobody. Finally the road ended at a teakwood gate with a high fence running for miles on either side of it." Mr. Hashiwara made one of his longer pauses. "It was a Zen Buddhist monastery," he said finally and turned and looked directly at Ralston. "Of course they have no Zen Buddhist monasteries in India but in this story we pretend they do. It was a Zen Buddhist monastery and the gatekeeper, who was a novice in the monastery and was somewhat bored keeping the gate, called out to the merchant immediately, 'Hello there, are you looking for salvation?'

"The merchant was tired and very hungry and besides he could not quite believe that he had invested all this pain and deprivation for nothing, and so he told the gatekeeper his story.

"'The ways of the world are pretty foolish,' the novice said. 'Some day I must tell you my story. But now you must come in and see the Zen master. He is not engaged in any contemplation now (as a matter of fact he is taking a sun bath) and he will hear your story and give you spiritual advice. The advice may be mysterious, but if you puzzle it out, you will understand.'

"So the novice who was gatekeeper opened the gate and the merchant came in and followed him up the road through the beautiful mountain country up to a shining lake on the shore of which the Zen master was sunbathing." Mr. Hashiwara pronounced the word *sunbath ing*. "The Zen master was a very old man and he wore no beard, but he was naked and looked very holy. At his right side was a walking staff of dongu wood and he was staring into the sun with his eyes half open. The merchant and the novice who was gatekeeper came up to the Zen master and stood before him. Before either of them could say a word to him however, the Zen master said to the merchant, 'Bend your head down.' The merchant bent his head down and the Zen master took up his stick of dongu wood. He hit the merchant over the head once with it and the merchant fell to the ground unconscious. He hit him the second time and the merchant's brains oozed upon the ground. He struck a third time and the skull split like a ripe pumpkin.

"The novice who was gatekeeper stared at the Zen master. 'Why did you do that, master?' he asked. 'This man wanted your advice and forgiveness. He had a story to tell, a story that was so sad that it almost broke my heart when he told it to me. But before he could say a word or I could explain his presence, you had taken your staff of dongu wood and swung it at his head three times and killed him. Why did you do that?'

"'He was standing in my light,' the Zen master said."

Mr. Hashiwara was silent. Ralston began applauding and the rest of the party (with the exception of one man who seemed to be asleep on the couch) rather nervously joined in. Mr. Hashiwara turned his head in Ralston's direction. "It is a very funny story, is it not?" he asked.

"Very funny," Ralston replied gravely.

"It is the story of the human condition," a very tall man with horn-rimmed glasses commented.

"Excuse me, no," Mr. Hashiwara said, lapsing, now the story was over, into his stage Japanese accent. "Is not a story of the human condition. Is a story of a man who commits incest with his daughter."

Ralston rose from the floor. "I'm going out to the kitchen to see if our host and hostess left us anything to drink," he announced. Quietly he made his way in that direction. The man in the horn-rimmed glasses seemed disposed to argue, "What I meant by the human condition —" and just before he passed out of the range of their sound Ralston could hear Mr. Hashiwara interrupt him with "You are speaking nonsense, sir. Please be quiet. The next story I wish to tell is about the cricket who wished to become a Bodhisattva."

So I have behaved unexpectedly, Ralston said to himself as
he moved outside the range of their voices, I have thrown the
ball to the flanking back instead of eating it, as I was expected
to, and now, when the least that could be expected of me is
that I stay in the backfield and help him with my blocking, I
have gone into the kitchen and intend to stay there and drink
several glasses of Slingbot's sherry — if I can find it — and be
proud of myself. The story itself, Ralston pursued his habit of
turning personal triumphs into literary allusions, was a warning to me. The Zen master (and everyone else in the story)
beat out the brains of the unfortunate merchant who committed incest with his daughter because he expected him. Only
the unexpected arrives.

"You managed that very well, I thought," a voice behind
him said. Ralston whirled, wondering if he had been talking to
himself. Seated alone at the small kitchen table with the rest
of the second bottle of sherry before him and a glass in his
hand was the bearded gentleman whom Ralston had tentative-
ly identified as the male half of the couple that would invite
him to dinner at their house in Sausalito. "Sit down and have
a glass of this vile sherry," the man said.

Ralston sat down and poured a glass silently. His triumph
was ruined. He decided to stare insultingly at the man's beard.
"You certainly got out from under," the man repeated.

"What did you think of Mr. Hashiwara's joke?" Ralston
asked merely for something to say.

"I'd heard it before — only then it was a Jewish story
about a man who fucked a goat." He extended his hand. "I'm
Peter Dawson. You don't have to look so uncomfortable. I
promise not to say a word about poetry."

"It was an embarrassing situation."

"Slingbot always manages them that way. He wants to
prove to people that he really has children so he lets them do
things like that. Janie's been sick at five of his parties."

"I knew Janie when she was born."

"Back when Madelaine was married to Tom Cross? That
was before my time. Things must have been different in those
days, I guess."

"I don't know enough of what they're like now to say."

"I don't suppose you do. You're a successful Eastern poet now. Is it true what Madelaine told me that you're planning to stay here for good now?"

"No."

"I didn't think so."

They both concentrated on drinking their glasses of sherry. I'm not a bit better for having left the room, Ralston thought. They have me trapped in the kitchen and now they'll come in one by one —

"I hear you tore up a poem of a friend of mine," Peter Dawson was saying.

"What?" Ralston was startled out of his bored aplomb for a moment and then quickly recovered. "Oh, the fish poet? Yes. He tore up a magazine of mine first though."

There was a sound of applause from the distant living room (Mr. Hashiwara had evidently finished his story about the cricket who wanted to be a Bodhisattva) and the two men drinking sherry in the kitchen felt for the first time a kind of friendship in the hope, not spoken but obviously shared, that Mr. Hashiwara would tell another story and keep the ravening mob from their not very interesting but comfortable refuge. It was more from this flickering sense of closeness than from any real curiosity that Ralston went on to ask, "Do you know this person Rue —"

"— Talcott —"

"— Rue Talcott very well?"

There was silence in the other room. Mr. Hashiwara had evidently begun another story. Ralston wondered vaguely what it would be about. Dawson pulled at his beard as if he wanted to make sure that it was really there. "My wife and I know Rue very well," he said. "He stayed with us when he first came in to town."

"What's his poetry like?" And why did he think of Mr. Hashiwara's merchant as soon as he had asked the question?

"I'm not a really good person to answer that question. I'm a painter myself, my wife's the poet. By the way, she especially wants me to ask you if you'll come out and have dinner with us some night. We live clear out in Marin County, but I'd be glad to drive in and pick you up."

"I'd be delighted to," Ralston heard himself saying.

"Fine. The poetry. I don't know how to describe it. Slingbot calls it authentic but he calls anything he approves of authentic. Rue's just a punk kid," (and Peter Dawson is all of twenty-four, beard and everything, Ralston thought from the distance of having passed thirty) "but his poems have something to them even I can see, sort of a combination of wild French stuff and the Wild West."

"I'm afraid I don't understand."

"Well it's hard to describe without making it sound corny. Freight trains and angels and small Southern jails and denunciations of the letters of the alphabet. And he was really in them. The freight trains and the jails, I mean."

"Looking for the last frontier?"

"No. This is real. He wasn't some Jew boy from New York who just wanted to see the country. He was born in a small railroad town in a godforsaken part of New Mexico and he ran away and started riding freights when he was thirteen. I know it sounds like something out of Davy Crockett but people still do it there, I guess. They don't need a depression to move them."

"But —"

"I know. I didn't believe much of what he told me at first either. I still don't believe all of it. He's got quite an imagination. But one time when we were walking down Market Street we ran into somebody he'd been to jail with in Waco and another time my wife and I met a guy at a party who said he'd taken care of Rue after he'd been beaten up in the freight yards in New Orleans. Little things like that, you know. But after a while you start to believe the rest of it."

"But the poetry —"

"Oh, he got it out of tin cans. I mean he'd steal paperbacks in drugstores — maybe comic books first but then paperbacks and then good paperbacks and he heard about Dante and Whitman and Rimbaud and then he invented a Dante and a Whitman and a Rimbaud of his own — all out of tin cans. Shit, I make him sound better than he is, I know that. But he's pretty good."

"How did he happen to come here?" Ralston was half fascinated by the impossible noble savage picture that the artist was painting but also half annoyed by the unique jealou-

sy he always felt when any other poet, dead or alive, was
being praised. "I mean The Birdcage is quite a hop, skip, and
a jump from Birmingham jail."

"I guess he must have read about San Francisco in one of
the paperbacks," Peter Dawson said. "He certainly made a
typical entrance. One evening I drove into town to open up the
6 Gallery — that's a cooperative art gallery out on Fillmore
and the artists take turns different nights of the week keeping
it open — and I found him inside sleeping on a couple of
chairs. He had picked the lock (which isn't any job because it's
a dimestore lock) and had been there all day. He showed me
the poem he had been writing before he explained anything."

"And so then he stayed with you?"

"Yes. Until we got sick of him. I'm infantile myself and one
infant around the house is enough. Besides he hated my wife's
poetry —" Peter Dawson ended the sentence with a smile.
"Anyway North Beach is much the best place for him."

"From what I've seen of it," Ralston said slowly, "it doesn't
seem like the best place for anyone."

"Well, he's happy there and people say he's writing his best
poetry. Anyway, it isn't my business. Did he really give you a
fish?"

"Yes," Ralston said. "A live fish." He poured the last of the
sherry into his glass.

"He's always doing things like that. One thing that was
good when he lived with us was that he made me feel glad
that I was a painter and had no literary imagination."

"It must have made your wife feel good too."

Peter Dawson's smile appeared briefly above his beard.
"She can take care of herself," he said. Ralston and he sat in
silence for a moment hearing the rustlings and the laughter in
the other room, and then the painter blurted out, as if it were
something he wanted to get over with, "Rue wants to see you."

"Has he caught another fish?" Ralston was suddenly tired
of the whole thing — not only the conversation about Rue, but
the whole trip to San Francisco, the whole search for a mysterious new kind of poetry. Talking to children about children —
it was a job for Anne not him.

"I was supposed to give you his message sooner, but I wanted to talk to you and see what you were like. He's waiting down at the bottom of the back stairs for you now."

"What?" Ralston was genuinely puzzled. Had he missed something that Dawson had said while he had been thinking? "I'm sorry. Who is waiting for me?"

"Rue wants to see you," the painter said patiently. "He's waiting down at the bottom of the back stairs."

"But why in bloody hell hasn't he come in? It doesn't matter if he hasn't been invited to the party. Madelaine and Slingbot aren't here."

"He was invited. He was specially invited. He just doesn't want to come in. He asked me to ask you to see him outside."

"Is there a secret password? Good Christ, why do we have to go through all this Tom Sawyer stuff? And why does he want to see me anyway?"

"Ask him." Dawson rose as if to dismiss the whole subject. "The door to the back stairs is through the pantry. I just gave you his message." He turned to go and then turned back as if he had forgotten something. "You will come to dinner with us, won't you? My number is in the Sausalito phone book. Call us when you're free to come to dinner. You don't have to give any warning. My wife's a good cook even if she is a poet." He winked at Ralston and left the room.

Was he joking, Ralston wondered. But if he was joking he was joking about everything. And besides painters don't make jokes like that. Jokes like that are products of the literary imagination — painters give you exploding cigars and itch powder. But if the whole thing was a joke his calling himself a painter might be a joke too. Ralston longed for the certainty of Mr. Hashiwara's universe where shaggy dogs were merely shaggy dogs, or Madelaine's where —. Nuts, ridiculous, *ausgeschlossen* — he would go down and see whether Rue was waiting for him, what on earth, if Rue was waiting for him, Rue really wanted — at the worst he could drink some of the half pint of bourbon at the bottom of the back stairs, if there really were back stairs and if there really was a bottom to them.

There really were back stairs and before he had reached the bottom of them a voice had called out, "Is that you?" and there was Rue sitting directly in his path a few steps from the bottom. "I suppose so," Ralston said, and then, cursing himself for his unsuccessful attempt at humor, sat down himself two steps above the boy.

Rue was silent. It was obviously Ralston's move to break the silence. He took the half pint of whiskey from his pocket, broke the seal, and unscrewed the cap. He handed it down. "Here, have a drink," he said.

Rue took the bottle, held it to his mouth for a minute, and then handed it back. There was no moon. Except for the light from the upstairs kitchen, almost complete darkness encircled them.

Ralston drank from the bottle himself. He was waiting for some sound, any sound. "I want you to read my poetry," the boy said.

"Why me? Why on earth do you pick me?" Ralston asked almost as if he were being persecuted, and then the school-teacher in him made him realize that he must have sounded rude and he added, "Your friend told me about the kind of poetry you write. You don't sound like you need anybody to advise you. Especially someone like me who probably wouldn't like what you're doing even if it was the greatest thing since Blake."

"I don't want advice." Ralston handed him the bottle and he swallowed again from it. "I don't even want you to like my poetry."

Ralston retrieved the bottle and took a long drink. "Then what *do* you want?" he asked.

"You're the only one who ever tore up one of my poems," the boy answered, as if, somehow, this made the relationship clear.

"Revenge? Proving that you're better than I thought you were?"

"You're not that stupid," the boy's voice had grown higher in pitch as the conversation went on. "You don't have to pretend that you're that stupid."

"I am." Ralston took another drink from the bottle without handing it to Rue. "I've already told you that I don't like riddles."

"Pretend you're another city," Rue said. "Pretend you're another city and I don't have to move even a mile to get to it. Do you understand at all?"

Ralston passed him the bottle. There was very little now left in it. "Why don't you just change cities?" he said. "Hop a freight train. People aren't cities and there's no getting around it."

"Here. Take it," Rue said. He handed a large manila envelope to Ralston in a gesture oddly more violent and more final between them than the tearing of the magazine had been.

"I don't promise to read your poetry," Ralston said. "I didn't come here to be a city for other people to visit. I don't like being treated as a symbol."

"I'll read your poetry," the boy said. "You can let me read your poetry."

"I haven't written it yet," Ralston said. "If I write the poem that I came here to write —" He knew that he was merely threatening himself. "Well, I'll take them. I won't promise to read them. I'll leave the manuscript off at The Birdcage when I'm through with it one way or another."

It was as if a pact had been concluded between them. Rue passed the half pint back to Ralston and Ralston swallowed the last of the whiskey left in it. He threw the bottle over the side of the stairs and it crashed into the courtyard below.

"I'll go back to the party now," Ralston said. "They're probably waiting for me."

"Come on with us. Peter and his wife and I are going to a real party. They'll be meeting me down here in a minute."

"No." Ralston got up, precariously tilting on the stair on which he had been sitting. "You were right at the beginning. We need neutral ground and I don't plan to sit on anybody else's stairs tonight. Goodbye." He turned, clutching the manila envelope, and started up the stairs.

"But when will I see you?" Rue called to his back. Ralston did not answer. He returned to the party, a headache, and the rest of the evening.

IV

When Ralston went back to his hotel room the next morning after having breakfasted on two cups of coffee and a San Francisco *Chronicle*, the desk clerk (slightly hostile as desk clerks always are in the presence of the unexpected) handed him two letters and a phone message. The telephone message was from Madelaine (who had called and wanted him to call back as soon as was possible) and the two letters were from Henry and Anne.

As he rode the elevator to his fourth floor room Ralston puzzled to himself which of the two letters he would open first. He had the same habit with letters that he had with food, he would save the best for last ("Eat your carrots, darling, and then you can have your dessert," his mother would say) and this would often, as now, plunge him into depths of indecision as to which letter would really be, or should really be considered to be, the best.

Not without some guilt, as he sat down in the one armchair in his room, he opened Anne's letter. After all he had talked to her on the telephone *after* she had sent this letter and there would be nothing — She had written it with a pen. That was odd. He began reading:

Dear Jim,

I am glad to have a chance to write a letter to you. It is so seldom that people in a relationship like ours get to say something to each other without being interrupted by remarks, since we know each other's train of thought so well, which completely disconcert us from what we are going to say. Oh dear, what a dreadful sentence! I'm sure that disconcert isn't a verb (or shouldn't be) and I haven't written anything without a typewriter since I was a first year student at Oberlin, but I want to he honest and *not* professional, and I'm sure I couldn't help telling lies if I used a typewriter.

Where was I? Oh yes, I was apologizing for writing you a serious letter. Seriously though, this is probably my

77

only chance to do it because I'll be leaving for Paris next
weekend and, *of course*, I'll have to write you about how
Europe looks after all these years. What I mean is, don't
think you'll have to reply to this as seriously as I wrote it
(and disconcert me) because this letter is a kind of therapy more for my benefit than yours — and you'll have
already phoned me before you get this letter — at least I
hope so — and you'll know that nothing is really wrong.

Schizophrenic children certainly cause a schizophrenic
prose style or maybe I feel that you're interrupting me
even though you aren't here, but I'd better go on now that
I've gotten started.

I suppose you don't really think I understand why
you've gone to San Francisco. You always have underesti-
mated my aesthetic perceptions, except at first when you
overestimated them and tried to convince me I could write
poetry. Remember? I do really understand most of your
reasons and since you're a husband and not a patient
(thank God) I think I have the right to comment on some
of them. Goodness, that last sentence seems to simply
bristle with hostility. Perhaps I'd better give up the pen
and go back to the typewriter. Or forget about the whole
thing. Or go on with what I'm trying to say.

Which is: you have a tendency to want things to be all
or nothing (a good thing in a way and, I'm sure, the very
reason I love you) and I'm afraid the fact that they won't
be all or nothing (the literary movement out there will
neither be as bad or as good as you hope it will be) will
puzzle you and frighten you and make you feel that you
have missed something. Am I telling you to put on your
overshoes or you'll catch cold, like a little mother? I suppose I am. But Jim, I love you as a person not as a poet
or a teacher or as a son and I suspect that I'm the only
person in the world (including yourself) that loves plain
simple Jim Ralston and, damn it, that gives me some
right to tell you to put on your overshoes or at least not to
go out in the rain stark naked. (That image probably
gives a clue to why I'm writing this letter. I suppose I
miss you physically more than I thought I did.)

Anyway, relax in San Francisco. Don't distrust yourself or try to put up traps saying if I don't do this or that it will certainly prove that I am not a great poet. I haven't the vaguest notion whether you are a great poet or not and only care because you care, but just remember that Shakespeare, Rimbaud, and Whitman are just as dead as any other corpses and no woman would look at them. Life, as I can never make clear to my children, only goes so far.

Have an affair in San Francisco, have five affairs or ten (how insincere that advice is subconsciously and how *sincere* that advice is consciously) but don't destroy yourself looking for more than a woman or life can give you.

This is all pretty silly. I promised myself when I married you that I'd never try to give you advice, but this is a sort of orgy of it. I'm relaxing and letting loose, too. What the hell, maybe all this advice refers to me.

I'll see you in a couple of months and we can have a fight over this letter. In a week I'll write to you from Paris and I promise that I won't bring along my pen. The Charles River is already full of green algae and Boston stinks of summer. I miss you.

Love,
Anne

Wholly untypical, thought Ralston. He had read the letter so fast that it was only after he was through with it that it occurred to him that it might easily have been (up to, say, the fourth paragraph) a letter telling Ralston that she was leaving him. He had not expected such a blow, a reassurance, no, face it, a message, from that direction and he felt like someone who had received a long distance call from his family (fortunately inconsequential) just when he was trying to keep the line open for an important local call.

The letter from Henry was shorter and more to the point:

Dear Jim:

I have been considering, as you might have guessed I would, the whole analogy of the football game in relation to your trip to San Francisco. There seemed to be a fallacy in it when you told it to me and now it seems to me that I can put my finger on it.

When you come to think of it, art is not very much like a football game. Consider for a minute your feelings when you attend a poetry reading or mine when I am present at a performance of Composer's Forum. There is a wholly different emotion. Our team can still have made twenty thousand first downs against Chaos and Noise University (a Virginia college) and we still can come away vaguely unsatisfied knowing that everything we heard was beautiful (immortal if you like) but still not as moved as if we had watched a single beefy fullback carry a football one yard toward the right-goal line at the right second.

I doubt if I'm putting this well. My mind works better in the realm of bibliography. But I remember when I was sixteen the shock I received when I began wondering whether I received greater personal satisfaction from eating a piece of chocolate pie or watching a performance of *Hamlet*. Being a middling honest man (le homme moyen veritable?) I admitted the chocolate pie and being more than middling shrewd, I suspected that the preference for chocolate pie would be permanent. It is.

Don't get me wrong. I would sacrifice, and have, a million chocolate pies for a single bar of music and at least a thousand for a performance of *Hamlet* but not for personal satisfaction. Football games and chocolate pies and all other really important pieces of satisfaction have to do with time — and art, whatever it has to do with, has precious little to do with satisfaction.

You mention Blake. Blake would have been a perfectly terrible quarterback — a good quarterback does not worry about the meaning of his act.

Why I feel impelled to warn you that you are acting on a bad analogy should be clear to you as a poet. The analogies one acts on are the greater part of one's life. To put a poem in the fourth quarter of a football game is as stupid as to assume that Caesar is a prime number.

Tom has written me that he is coming to Berkeley for a few days. He has the summer off from teaching just like you do. You will want to see him.

I am not sure that Blake is the right analogy either. One does not ask to see angels.

Your friend,
Henry

It is creepy, Ralston thought, how sometimes everything combines to give you an absolutely unnecessary moral lesson. He put both letters in an empty dresser drawer, resolving not to forget that he had put them there when he moved out of the hotel room (he must look for an apartment today, Anne, Anne of the phone call, was right) and looked over at the envelope of Rue's poetry that was lying on the night stand. He had not looked at it. He would not look at it until he had written at least one fourth-quarter (yes, damn Henry, fourth-quarter) poem of his own. He had, he now for the first time remembered, spent from one o'clock to five o'clock of this very morning trying to write one. This in itself was a revealing discovery. He was not only hung-over, he was sleepy. This somehow — the fact that he had only slept five hours — explained everything — even the unopened envelope of poetry, even the letters. He would find an apartment or a room today, but first (and here the certainty that a third creepy unnecessary moral lesson would be the result of it intruded on his newborn relief) but first he must call Madelaine.

Madelaine was home. "Oh Jim, I'm so glad you called. Arthur and I must have just missed you. We got back to the party a little after twelve."

"How is Janie?" Ralston ventured.

"Oh, there was nothing wrong with Janie. Nothing except the vomiting. It turns out that she'd dipped the thermometer in her tea while we weren't watching when we took her temperature. She'd read about it in a book."

"She seems to be an annoying child."

"I think she is. She's gotten terribly spoiled in the last few years. But Arthur won't hear a word against her. He's much fonder of her than he is of his own children. Did you have a good time at the party?"

"No."

Madelaine giggled. "I didn't really think you would. Was it too awful after we left?"

"Yes."

"I hear you and that nice Japanese man kept the guests entertained."

"He told stories and then later we had an argument about how to cook rice."

"How to cook rice?"

"There was some symbolism in it that escapes me this morning."

"I hear you spent half the evening out on the back steps with Rue Talcott. You haven't gotten that way since you've been married, have you?"

"If you mean either avant-garde or homosexual, no." Ralston's voice had taken on a sharper edge. "You wanted me to call you about something, didn't you?"

"Goodness. You don't have to bite my head off. I just thought that since the children are all at school and Arthur is off on a civil liberties case, you might want to come over and have tea with me."

"A civil liberties case?" Ralston asked, less because he was interested than because he wanted to delay a decision on the afternoon visit to Madelaine and all it would (or wouldn't) imply.

"A nice Negro boy (although I don't know why I call him a boy since he's almost as old as we are) named Washington Jones who makes wire sculpture. Some woman accused him of attacking her last night —"

"Washington Jones," Ralston interrupted. "So his name really was Washington Jones."

"What are you talking about?" Madelaine asked angrily.

"I think I know him."

"You couldn't. He wasn't at the party. That's just the trouble. He was at another party and this awful girl (she's a Bulgarian refugee) claims he attacked her and gave her a black eye and sprained her arm on the way home. Arthur's at the police station now trying to raise bail. He's going to call in the American Civil Liberties Union."

"He's big enough to sprain anyone's shoulder, but I'll admit he doesn't look the type," Ralston said, attempting before the conversation should go any further to shatter this nonsensical assumption of Madelaine's that anyone he knew in this town he would know through her.

"Then you do know him! But I don't see how you could. He wasn't in town when you lived here before."

"I met him in The Birdcage the first day I was in town. The day I met Rue."

"You really know him." Ralston, in spite of the fact that he was listening over a receiver, felt he could hear the wheels turning in Madelaine's head. "But that's wonderful. That's the other thing that Arthur is looking for. Character witnesses. And you're a professor in an Eastern college and there won't be the prejudice against you that there is against Arthur."

"I don't know him. I *met* him. I talked to him for about ten minutes in a bar."

"That doesn't matter. They won't ask you how long you knew him. They're only trying to find people to testify to his character. I'll call Arthur at the police station and he'll call you back in about five minutes."

"No —" but Madelaine had already hung up.

Ralston thought of leaving the room to avoid the ensuing call but decided that Slingbot, if nothing else, was rational, and he could easily explain to him the mistake that Madelaine was making. Besides, this, if only for the space of two phone calls, was an involvement, and involvement was the only answer to the letters that Anne and Henry had written to him.

As he waited, Ralston idly wondered whether he would have accepted Madelaine's invitation if the idiotic mistake that had come from his delaying question had not gotten in the way. He suspected he would. Madelaine's sexual attractiveness was the kind that increased rather than diminishing when one realized what a bitch and how stupid she was. And she would have arranged, he felt sure, another interruption at the crucial moment fully as final and embarrassing as Janie. But still —

Arthur called him in not much more than five minutes. He was breezy and businesslike. "Hello, Jim. I hear your're interested in helping our mutual friend out of his predicament."

"I tried to make Madelaine understand that he's not even an acquaintance. I merely met him in a bar. I'm sorry she put you to all this trouble of calling."

"Oh, it's no trouble, " Slingbot became even more charming.

"I wanted to thank you anyway for helping us when we had to leave the party. I hear you did a wonderful job. Everybody liked you."

"Uh —"

"The thing is, I have another favor to ask. I've got Washington out on bail now —"

"How did you ever raise enough money to pay bail on a rape case?"

"A rape case? It's not a rape case. Where did you ever get that idea?"

"Madelaine."

"Oh. Madelaine reads sex into everything. No. This Sonia Liebowitz claims that he hit her in the face a number of times after he drove her home. It's a simple assault case. Legal type assault."

"Madelaine said that she was a Bulgarian refugee. Liebowitz doesn't sound Bulgarian."

"She changed her name to Liebowitz. There are a number of odd things about her. I think she was a Fascist during the war. Anyway, she's the type that would blame a Negro for anything that happened to her. They're classical father figures."

"The women?" Ralston was genuinely puzzled.

"No. Negroes. Ask your wife some time."

"I still don't see what you want *me* to do."

"I tried to get the Civil Liberties Union to take the case, but they're too lily-livered to touch it. But I've got hold of a good lawyer, Gerald Simpson — he broke with the CP at the same time I did — and he's going to take the case without charging a fee. What we hope now is that the thing won't even come to court — that she'll withdraw her charges. That's where you come in."

"But I don't even know her."

"That's just the point. If we can show her and her lawyer that we have a lot of character witnesses for Washington —

and that's the crux of the case, it's merely her word against his, no evidence or witnesses — she's almost certain to withdraw her charges. I've been trying to find other people that know him, but you're the best so far. It's not a question of testifying. It's just a question of pretending that you're ready to testify."

"Is there any chance that Jones really did beat her up?"

"Of course not. But even if he did, the bitch probably deserved it. The point is that if it ever comes to court, Washington will be up against all the prejudice against his race in this vicious bloody town. Already the sergeant that booked him called him a nigger."

"I didn't realize that there was that much racial feeling in San Francisco."

"Much racial feeling!" Slingbot almost shouted. "I could tell you stories — Anyway what I want you to do is to jump in a cab and meet me on the courthouse steps. Washington is with me right now. I'll buy you a drink and we can figure out what we're going to tell the lawyer."

"Tell the lawyer?"

"Well, Jerry has gotten awfully respectable in the last few years. I don't know how he'd take it if we told him that you were merely pretending to be a character witness. He might not want to know. That's why we have to talk it over before we see him."

"I don't really know if I want to get mixed up in this," Ralston said.

"Oh, for Christ's sake, man!" Slingbot's voice vibrated through the telephone. "Don't you see that it will be fun. And put the squares down too. Something like this is just what you need to keep your mind occupied while you adjust to San Francisco."

"But I don't want —"

"Anyway come down here and talk about it. Talking about it won't commit you to anything. If I could think of anyone else with a respectable university background — You'll be there in fifteen minutes, won't you?"

Ralston found himself saying yes. Afterwards he blamed it on the two letters he had received.

There was, nevertheless, a certain amount of moral blackmail involved, Ralston thought to himself after he had finally
located a taxi, gotten to the Hall of Justice, and was now
waiting for an Arthur Slingbot and a Washington Jones who
were nowhere to be seen. He had a guilty secret. He had spent
seven of the first ten years of his life in Texas. It was conceivable that Slingbot knew this. And even if Slingbot did not
know this, the moral position was difficult.

(Ralston, who had left Houston, which was not even then
a very typical Texas town, when he was ten, nevertheless had
received a traumatic and lasting impression when he witnessed an incident on a streetcar in the Los Angeles his par-
ents had moved back to. A Southerner — probably a Virginian
or Carolinian from his speech but certainly from no further
west than the Mississippi River — had started to make a
scene about a Negro who had taken a seat next to him. He
had begun muttering in a low but audible voice, "Damn ni-
gras. What's the matter with this town where I have to sit
next to a damn pushing nigra?" and the people on the streetcar instead of siding with him, or, as Ralston's Houston experience would have led him to expect, keeping embarrassed
silence, had instead raised equally audible murmurs against
the Southerner — "Damn Okies, why don't they go back where
they came from if they don't like it here?", "Ought to turn 'em
back at the border when they try to get in.", "Bury 'em at the
border and give Oklahoma back to the Indians." — the Virginian left the streetcar at the next stop and the Negro was
smiling. Ralston's moral sense had not been outraged — Houston was not Texas — but he was very careful after this in
trying to lose the Southernness of his accent and, like an anti-
Semitic Jew, to be the first to yell "Okie" and to lead the
attack on all things Southern.)

But, Ralston thought, if I refuse to do something silly like
being a character witness for someone I don't really know and
Slingbot discovers that I spent part of my childhood in Texas
(and, he just remembered, there was always Madelaine to tell
him) he'll blow up the story until he's convinced everybody
that I'm a special emissary from the Ku Klux Klan. Ralston
could remember a few years ago when the University of California invited an inoffensive Southern poet (a friend of Tate

and Ransom) to read in a lecture series what a storm Slingbot managed to cause. The man, inappropriately named Philander Green, was a Fascist, was a defender of lynching (in fact, Slingbot implied, had himself probably participated in several), was furthermore a very bad, very academic poet, and never should have been considered, much less invited. The University of California, being even larger and more corpulent than Slingbot, was unmoved by his reasoning, but the poetic community boycotted the reading almost to a man.

Slingbot's feeling on the matter was not a bit like Ralston's. He had no Southern background to overcome. (Ralston believed that he had been born somewhere in New Jersey and knew that he had lived in Pittsburgh, was the center of Pittsburgh's artistic life, before he came to San Francisco.) Nor was this merely a crotchet like his violent hatred of the Catholic Church or the Stalinists. It was more, Ralston decided, an attempt to join the Negro race as a gifted amateur might join a jazz band for a number. Slingbot delighted in using words that he claimed only Negroes used, in telling Negro jokes to Negroes that Negroes tell to other Negroes, in wearing a perpetual and rather authentic blackface whenever Negroes were present. And yet there was no element of even reversed prejudice in all this and it was not offensive. But it could be damnably annoying.

The subject of Ralston's fears was now walking out of one of the doors and onto the steps. He was wearing a dark red shirt and a black tie with dirty gray flannels. Beside him, just as tall but looking incredibly thin beside him, was Washington Jones, impeccably clad in Brooks Brothers charcoal gray. Jones greeted Ralston first, "Hello, man. I haven't seen you since you threw away that fish."

Ralston smiled and extended his hand — something he would never have done if it had not been for his previous train of thought. It always embarrassed him when people who never shook hands with anybody shook hands with Negroes as a sort of flag of truce. Now he was doing it. To make up for it slightly he also shook hands with Slingbot.

"Let's go over to the bar across the street," Slingbot said. "We three want to have a talk before the lawyer comes."

They crossed the street. Ralston, in the middle of the trio, felt especially small and especially purposeless. "I'm not sure what we're going to talk about," he said.

"My vicious attack on the person of Sonia Liebowitz," Washington Jones said. "Didn't the man tell you?"

When they seated themselves in the small bar, Slingbot asked if beer was all right for everybody and Ralston, remembering the eighty-five cents he had paid in taxi fare, said no he wanted a bourbon and water. His aggressive gestures toward Slingbot, he thought to himself wryly, had almost wholly to do with alcohol.

"The point," Slingbot said, paying for the drinks and taking over the chairmanship of the discussion in the process, "is this. We have to frighten this hysterical female — and her lawyer if she has one — out of pressing charges. There's no reason for this even to go to court."

"I don't see why you're worried," Ralston objected. "As you said on the telephone, it's merely her unsupported word against his. There's no chance of anyone making a case even if it gets to court."

"There might be prejudice."

"What Mr. Slingbot means," Washington Jones interjected, "is that I've been in trouble before. I had a suspended sentence last year for possession of two joints of marijuana and I once served a two-months sentence for assault in New York."

"When he was a mere child," Slingbot said. "A mere child in a slum jungle."

"What happened?" Ralston asked.

"I hit a cat over the head with a beer bottle." Jones paused and smiled. "He said something about my mother."

"So you see," Slingbot said. "They'd give him a hard time if he went to court. All sorts of prejudice. Besides that, all of the three judges the case would be likely to go before are Catholic and you know how anti-Negro the Catholics are."

"I thought the Catholic Church was supposed to be less prejudiced than any other," Ralston said. "Haven't they —"

"I know," Slingbot interrupted. "The hierarchy of the American Catholic Church pretends to support the Negro. They're very clever. But you should see the record of the Church in Belgian Congo."

All three drank in silence for a moment. Finally Ralston said, "Let me see if I understand what you want me to do. You want me to pretend to your lawyer and to the girl if necessary that I've known Mr. Jones for a long time and that I think highly of his character."

"That's right."

"What happens when somebody discovers that I've only been in town for a week?"

"You could have known him in New York. He only came into town two years ago. You probably have seen his wire sculptures in some galleries in New York. Besides you don't have to say that you've known him for a long time — just that you'll testify for him as a character witness."

"Which I won't."

"That's right. If you tell them that there'll be no trial and nobody will have to testify to anything. When the Liebowitz girl discovers that you and I are willing to go on the stand for Washington, she'll drop all her charges. After all, she doesn't know about his police record."

"Doesn't she?" Ralston turned to Jones.

"I don't think so," the tall Negro answered slowly. "She may know about the pot rap, but she smokes it herself and that wouldn't impress her. She's a funny chick."

"She's an hysterical pathological liar," Slingbot said.

"She's pretty mixed up," Jones said. "Anyway, Mr. Ralston, it would be a real swinging thing if you'd do this for us."

It seemed less swinging to Ralston every moment. "But don't you have some kind of alibi?" he asked. "Can't you prove that you couldn't have beaten her up at the time she says you did?"

"I don't know whether I have an alibi or not," Washington Jones said. "I don't think I do."

Slingbot for the first time looked nervous. "We've already gone into that," he said sharply. "You were home asleep but can't prove it."

"No." Jones turned to face him with dignity. "If Mr. Ralston is going to stick his neck out for me, I want to tell him the truth. Let him decide if he believes me."

Slingbot shrugged his shoulders.

"I didn't tell the police any of this. That would have been stupid. But you," Jones said, turning to Ralston, "certainly have a right to know." He paused, waiting for Ralston to make some noise of agreement, but he was silent. "Sonia claims this happened at about 4:30 this morning. We had all been at this crazy party together. Your friend Rue was there. He says that he invited you but that you put the whole thing down."

Again Jones paused. This time Ralston spoke. "He might put it that way," he said.

Jones smiled. Slingbot fiddled with his drink. "Anyhow," Jones said, "I was out of it before I got there. I'd been on dexies for two days solid — the no sleep jazz — and I'd been lushing it up since early that morning. I must have passed out or something around midnight. The next thing I knew I was in bed in my pad at around six or so and the fuzz was knocking at the door."

"People saw him pass out," Slingbot said.

"Yes. I was supposed to have been stretched out on the couch at the party. But I must have crawled away. They say I disappeared at about two."

"Exactly what does the Liebowitz girl claim you did to her?" Ralston asked.

"She says I picked her up in a car in front of the party when she was leaving and offered her a ride home. That was supposed to be at about 4:30. And after I'd taken her part of the way home, I beat her up instead."

"How do you know you didn't?"

"That's the crazy thing. I don't even know how to drive. And there weren't any cars missing around the party. And I wasn't in any condition to breathe much less drive a car. It must just have been some other cat that looked like me. Sonia was pretty drunk herself, and, like Mr. Slingbot says, she's a little crazy."

"Tell him what the fuzz did when they busted you," Slingbot said.

"Aw, they cuffed me around a bit and said that they weren't going to have no niggers beating up lily white American motherhood. But they were real nice to me at the station. They let me call up Mr. Slingbot. I went to NYU Law School for two years," he added, winking at Ralston.

"And you don't remember anything about how you got home or when you left the party?"

"Not a thing. Of course I didn't tell the fuzz that. But I don't remember a single thing."

"Probably half the people that were at the party can't remember what they were doing between two and six in the morning," Slingbot said positively.

"Sure. Everybody was pretty high." Washington Jones winked again at Ralston. "Probably Rue put on blackface and did it himself."

"Well, that's the story," Slingbot said. Ralston clicked around the ice in his empty highball glass, but Slingbot did not hear him. "That's the story. Will you help us?"

"I don't like to commit myself before a lawyer, even yours," Ralston said. "After all it's so easy to check that I haven't known him for more than a week. I'd like to help. If there was something else I could do."

"I know just how you feel," Jones said, not sounding a bit hurt or disappointed. "I don't like this lawyer jazz myself. There is one thing you could do. Sonia's a little crazy but down underneath she's a good chick. If someone would go and talk to her and explain the mess she's causing, we might be able to stop this whole scene cold, without lawyers or anything. If you could go and talk to her —"

Ralston said, "Why me?" and Slingbot said, "I'll go" simultaneously.

"No, Mr. Slingbot," Jones said. "It can't be any of my friends — I mean my old friends — she wouldn't even listen. But Mr. Ralston here doesn't belong to any of the politics of this town. He can listen to her story and sympathize with her and show her how she's doing wrong. If you would —"

"I'd be glad to," Ralston said. He felt relieved and a little disappointed at having gotten off so cheaply. "Do you know what hospital she's at?"

"Oh, she's not in any hospital," Slingbot said. "They sent her home. I checked that first thing. She was just bruised up a bit." He paused for a moment. "You know, that is an excellent idea. The fact that Jim would take so much trouble to visit her would imply that he's an old friend of yours without actually stating it. Subtle. Damnably subtle." He turned to Ralston. "Let her know that you're a college professor."

"Just play it straight, Mr. Ralston," Jones said hurriedly. He extended his hand. "And thanks."

Ralston left the bar with Sonia's address (supplied by Washington Jones) in his pocket. It was on the 1200 block of Kearny which would mean, Ralston knew, an exhausting walk half way up to the top of Telegraph Hill. But he was out of it — and with honor. And in, also, as far as he wished, into a new involvement with new people's lives. And Rue (the figure of whatever poetry he was) had been at the party.

North Beach is neither a beach or particularly north. It is a slanted valley between three heavily populated and expensive hills which is separated from the bay (on the two sides it approaches it) by a forbidding district of industries and warehouses. Though it does not feel a bit like a valley (it slants upward from the end of it at the Hall of Justice where Ralston was starting from) it retains one of the basic psychological features of a valley — the feeling of being overshadowed. Wherever you are in it, there is something, on one side or the other, which is higher than you are.

The side of The Beach that Ralston started from (it is usually called The Beach by its residents because it is unquestionably not a beach and one could argue that it was relatively north) contained, besides the Hall of Justice, the central police station, some new interior decoration shops, some old bars which were, in their way, the last remnants of the old Barbary Coast (which was also not a coast), and a new store specializing in avant-garde paperback books. It is quite depressing. It is sometimes known as the "old district" as at one time, because one supposes of the immediate availability of its prostitutes, it was the center of the paleolithic Bohemia of Jack London, George Sterling, and Ambrose Bierce. Later, in the 1930s, its further edge toward the "new district," at the place where the paperback shop now stands, was the center of the innocent and vaguely proletarian Bohemia of William Saroyan and John Steinbeck. During the Second World War both the Chinese and the Bohemians crossed Broadway into the "new district" (much to the displeasure of the Italians who, up to then, had been its only inhabitants) and upper Grant St.

became filled with bars like The Birdcage and the lower reaches of Russian and Telegraph Hills (where the houses were too old or too Italian to be remodeled into expensive apartments) were filled with the newest, and perhaps the least exciting versions of Bohemian living.

Ralston, although post-Second World War himself, felt a vague nostalgia as he walked up Columbus through the "old district." He at least had known people to whom Izzy Gomez's bar had been as real as The Birdcage, who remembered and talked of The Black Cat as the only left-bank bar outside of Paris. Looking at all of it now was as painful as walking through an abandoned amusement park.

But he soon passed Broadway and the regions of nostalgia and discontent. He stopped for a drink in one of the "new" bars on upper Grant St. He dawdled. His errand was not unpleasant (he felt rather like a sympathetic character from one of the novels of Henry James) but he was in no hurry to complete it. It did not occur to him to ask himself the exact words of gentle calculated diplomacy that he was going to speak to Sonia. He felt, like the geography of The Beach itself, that they were already written for him.

It was already four o'clock when Ralston started climbing halfway up the steep hill to the address that had been given to him. Sonia's apartment (mysteriously listed as 22½ on the register) was extremely difficult to find. He lost himself several times in the maze of backstairs, and when he finally located number 22, he found that there was only a communal toilet next to it. 22½ turned out to be seven doors and one level away.

22½, when he found it, was unmistakable. There was a large visiting card with Sonia Liebowitz printed on it in gothic letters tacked to the door. He knocked. "Come in, " a voice with a slightly foreign accent shouted. "The door's open." Ralston could hear the sounds of jazz in the background — modern jazz of some sort. He opened the door.

The door must have been quite thick, because the sound of the music (which came from a record player) almost deafened Ralston as he stepped inside. It was a one-room apartment — an armchair, a sink, and a daybed. On the daybed was a figure so swathed in bandages that Ralston, at first, could hardly determine its sex. "Excuse me," he said, "are you —"

The figure put a bandaged hand to an unbandaged mouth. "Shhh!" she said. "Capstan's blowing." With the same hand she indicated the one chair in the room.

Ralston sat down. A drum solo began to emerge from the background. It went on for a long time, and then the record stopped. Sonia, by now he was sure it was Sonia, turned and looked at him suspiciously. "I don't know you," she said.

"This is all very unofficial," Ralston began, wondering why he did not feel more disconcerted, more embarrassed.

She screamed out this time. "I don't know you. What right have you to force your way into my room? I will call the manager."

This last statement (which seemed a particularly empty threat as the manager, if there was one, would, Ralston felt, have as hard a time finding room 22½ as he had had) was delivered in a lower voice. She leaned back and stared at him with small shrewd eyes. "I'm a friend of Washington Jones," Ralston said in his coldest, most formal manner (he was enjoying this). "I want to talk to you about this unfortunate misunderstanding."

Her voice became a scream again. She clutched at the bandages on her face and arms. "Is this a misunderstanding? Is that? Is that? You Americans are so in love with violence that you call these misunderstandings?"

"I was referring to your mistaken identification of Mr. Jones as the man who attacked you," Ralston said. Slingbot, for once, was right. This woman was an hysteric and had to be handled firmly. "You had all been drinking. It was very late at night. I'm sure that some Negro that looked vaguely like Mr. Jones did attack you. You probably didn't see what was happening very clearly."

Sonia, surprisingly, laughed. "You Americans," she said. "All Negroes look alike to you. All people who are not pure-blooded Anglosaxons look alike to you. Not to me. I can see beneath the color of the skin. I am not prejudiced."

Ralston was somewhat taken aback by the turn of the argument. "If you are not prejudiced —" he began.

"Go back to your atomic bombs," she screamed. (Ralston noticed, even in his confusion, that the trick of her conversation was to start talking in a scream and to end the series of statements in a low, sincere, rational voice.) "I do not believe in your violence. I can recognize one American from another and they are all the same whether black or white-colored. They all want to drive fast in cars or throw bombs or hurt people. Your Washington Jones will go to jail. Sure I saw him."

"But he doesn't even drive a car." Ralston noticed with alarm that her style of conversation was beginning to have an effect on his own.

"You think he can't drive a car just because he's a Negro. Poof, you Americans! Negroes like to drive cars just like anyone else."

Things were getting more confused by the minute. "I mean that he personally can't drive," Ralston said. "He doesn't know how."

"If he can't drive, how did he drive me home?" Sonia screamed triumphantly. "Would you like some tea?"

Ralston welcomed a diversion at this point. "I'll make it for you," he said. He looked around the room for some kind of hotplate.

"We must use hot water from the faucet," Sonia said sadly. "The landlord does not allow the use of cooking implements. But the water is very hot."

Ralston removed some dirty dishes from the small washbasin and washed out two cups. He let the hot water run for a long time. Finally he filled the cups with it and put a teabag in each. Her handed a cup to Sonia.

"Thank you," she said. "We must wait a minute for the tea is slow to dissolve."

"About the car," Ralston began.

"I am very sorry," Sonia said. "I do not talk business during tea. It is an old European custom. I wish I had some wafers to offer you."

They sat in silence, Ralston swirling his teabag in the lukewarm water. Sonia finally broke the silence. "How did you like Capstan's record?" she asked.

Ralston tried to drink some of the tea. It tasted like hot water. "It was fine," he said.

"They will kill him, of course," Sonia said. "They will kill him like they killed their Charlie Parker and all of the others. When I first came to America I knew the Bird."

Ralston, not knowing what else to do, nodded.

She continued, "When I knew the Bird he was living in a small room in the Greenwich Village and nobody visited him. They wouldn't give him jobs anymore because he was too far gone on heroin. I brought him soup. Later that year he died."

Ralston cared very little for Charlie Parker and did not know what to do with the story. "Did you like jazz before you came to America?" he asked.

"Always. Always the real jazz. Of course in Sofia I could hear in mainly in records. Only occasionally did some good combo come to play for us. But when I escaped from the Communist scum and went to Stockholm I had an affair with a Negro bandleader named Johnny Wanes and traveled over Europe with him." Ralston must have shown by his expression that he was startled, for she suddenly screamed at him, "Ah, you are shocked, little man! You can have a Negro for a friend but I cannot have one for a lover. So condescending!"

Ralston was about to explain, or supposed he was about to explain, that he did not in the least care if she slept with every Negro bandleader in Europe, but just as he began to speak, the door (which was behind him) opened. "So you finally got back," Sonia screamed, looking directly over Ralston's head. Ralston turned his head. There, standing in the doorway with a paper sack in his hand, was Rue.

Rue was surprised. He put the paper bag on the floor (there didn't seem to be any table) and stared at Ralston. "I didn't know you were a friend of Sonia's," he said.

"Ah," Sonia threw back her unbandaged arm dramatically. "So you know this person. He won't tell me his name. He just sits there drinking my tea and making stupid remarks."

Rue seemed strangely constrained. Ralston, both puzzled and pleased by this, said merely, "I've been sent to Miss Liebowitz as a kind of ambassador."

Rue looked uncertainly at him, then his face cleared. "Oh," he said. "Slingbot called you. The fight Sonia had with Judge."

Sonia turned her bandaged face, coquettishly Ralston felt, toward Rue. "I have told you, boy. It was not a fight. That monster brutally attacked me. And who is this chi-chi friend of yours who comes to visit me and tells me nothing?"

Ralston waited half amused and half angry. He would let Rue carry the ball. Rue, however, was silent and made an elaborate business of taking a quart of beer out of the paper bag and looking for an opener. Sonia was also silent. She closed her eyes and, somewhat theatrically, leaned back on the daybed. Rue found the opener, opened the quart of beer, and very thoroughly washed out a glass. He poured beer into it and handed it to Ralston. "Here," he said. "You probably need this after Sonia's tea."

"Thank you, " Ralston said.

Sonia opened her eyes and raised herself to a sitting position. "Baby," she screamed, "Who is this mome? You give him the only glass in the house for his beer."

"We can use the teacups," Rue said, emphasizing his statement by collecting the cups and beginning to wash them. "You shouldn't break so many glasses. By the way," he said, turning to Ralston, "have you read my poems yet?"

Ralston, who did not relish being forced to speak at this point, was rescued by a series of threatening and incomprehensible sounds that started to rise from Sonia's lips. It must, he thought, have been Bulgarian. After almost a half minute of these, she said quietly, "What I was saying is that you both fuck pigs. Stop playing with me, baby. Who is this man and what does he want with you?"

Rue turned to her. "I told you that all hell would break loose when you blew the whistle on Judge. He's Jim Ralston. Slingbot's sent him over here to bring you to your senses."

"My senses," Sonia screamed. "I was beaten senseless by that maniac and now you want me brought to my senses."

"If I know you, you probably hit him over the head with a bottle first," Rue said. "It takes a great deal to get Judge angry."

"What I was trying to tell her," Ralston said, feeling this was the time, if there ever was one, for affirming that he still was in the room, "is that she seems to have made a mistake. This Washington Jones can't even drive a car."

"Drive a car?" Rue was puzzled.

"She claims he drove her home before he beat her."

"Is this true, Sonia? You didn't tell me anything about driving home with him."

"I thought you were more interested in my injuries than in the exact details of how I received them," Sonia said tightly.

"But whose car did he drive you home in?"

"Unfortunately I did not check the register number. I will always do that when I drive home with one of your friends again. Believe me."

"You see," Ralston said, delighted to fan the flames, "we think she may have made a mistake."

"Mistake!" Sonia shouted at Rue. "I do not know your friend the Judge as you call him! He has drunken my tea, smoked my cigarettes, stolen my beer. I have even slept with him. And I do not recognize him. It is all a mistake, Poof!"

"I don't see how she could have made a mistake about it," Rue said to Ralston. "But on the other hand I've never seen Judge drive a car." He turned to Sonia. "Are you sure you haven't invented all this?" he asked.

Sonia began to cry. Heavy, deep, wheezing sobs. Ralston sat there in silent embarrassment, for the first moment not enjoying the whole thing. "I know you don't love me," she said.

Ralston got up from his chair. "I guess I'd better go."

Rue was still standing, pouring beer into the two teacups. "Don't be silly," he said. "This is the time to get everything straightened out."

"And me straightened out too," Sonia screamed. "I confess. I confess. Nothing happened at all." She pointed to her bandaged arm and face. "I have just cut myself shaving." She began sobbing more deeply and less, it seemed to Ralston, realistically.

"I think I'd better come back some other time," Ralston said. He edged toward the door.

Rue stopped him. "No," he said quietly and finally. He handed a teacup of beer to Sonia and began sipping from the other himself. "Look, Sonia," he said. "I'm not against you. Nobody's against you. We just have to know what happened."

Sonia, somewhat surprisingly, stopped crying. She took a sip of beer. "I will tell you everything," she said. "And then you two beasts will go off into the flowers together and laugh at poor Sonia and say what a good thing it is that your friend the Judge as you call him has beaten her up."

Rue began to say something, but Sonia, in the loudest voice Ralston had heard her use, shouted, *"Tais-toi!"* She then began, in a quiet and almost academic voice, to recite her story.

She had been waiting, sometime after three in the morning, outside the party for a taxicab. ("That was after you had thrown a glass of wine in my face," Rue said. "By the way, how were you planning to pay for the cab?" "I don't give all my money to you," Sonia said. "I keep some for myself.") And Washington Jones, evidently very drunk, had come by in a car and offered her a ride. ("No, I do not remember what make and model car it was. All your American cars look like metal-covered suppositories.") Being very angry with Rue ("I did not care where baby stayed last night. It was not going to be with me.") she was glad to accept the ride. Jones had been moody and very drunk ("He did not say a single word to me and drove in the wrong directions.") and when he had driven her about a block from her house he suddenly slapped her across the face with his fist and began to beat her. ("What had you said to him?" Rue asked. "I do not remember. Something pleasant.") She had finally managed to escape him and get out of the car, but he caught her and when he hit her again she fell and broke her arm. She began screaming and he drove away in the car. A few minutes later a passing motorist noticed her on the sidewalk. ("Why did you stay that long on the sidewalk?" Rue asked. "I thought both my legs were broken too," Sonia said calmly.) The motorist drove her to the emergency hospital.

The recital impressed Ralston. One point bothered him, however. "Jones didn't say a single word to you the whole time?"

Sonia turned to Rue, smiling. "The little man still thinks I made a mistake in identity. Tell him how well I know your friend that you call the Judge."

Rue looked worried. "She knows him well enough," he said to Ralston. He turned to Sonia, "But I still don't see why you blew the whistle on him. Even if he flipped that badly, it's no reason to send him to jail."

"I hate violence," Sonia screamed. "I hate your American violence. Men should not be allowed to beat defenseless women."

Rue laughed, "It's me you're talking to, Sonia. You're about as defenseless as a bulldozer."

Sonia screamed "Haha haha" several times in an hysterical mimic of Rue's laugh. "It is very funny." She pointed with her undamaged hand to the bandages. "And who will pay for these? And who will pay for the doctor's care? Will you pay for them with my money? Will your friend Mr. Ralston who wears a pinstriped suit and drinks my tea and my beer pay for them? Haha haha!"

"She's right, you know," Rue said. "All this is going to be very expensive."

"I'm afraid I'll have to be going," Ralston said. "All I came here for was to make sure that she was really convinced that Jones did the beating and that she wanted to prosecute him. I really don't know who's right and who's wrong." He swallowed the last of his beer and stood up.

"Sonia," Rue said. "You'd drop the charges if Judge paid the doctor bills, wouldn't you?"

"The doctor bills! And what about the time I will lose on my novel because I have a broken arm? And what about the pain and the suffering? He would have to pay me more than the doctor bills. He would have to pay me thousands of dollars."

"Jones doesn't look as if he owns thousands of dollars," Ralston said coolly. "He's hardly the person to obtain a fortune from."

"As a matter of fact," Rue said, "Judge's family is supposed to own a string of shoe stores in Connecticut. They send him money every month. He could probably afford to pay something."

"If he's guilty," Ralston said, feeling more and more that he was in a false position.

"I will send him to jail for twenty years," Sonia said. "I will not accept a cent of his dirty money. Tell him that."

"Sonia will change her mind in a few minutes," Rue said. "Do talk to Slingbot and have him talk to Judge and see if they can't work something out."

"I'll give him your message," Ralston said. "Now I have to go. Thank you both for the tea and the beer."

"Wait," Rue said. "Have another glass of beer and talk to me. Have you read my poetry yet?"

"I haven't had time," Ralston said. "You only gave it to me last night. Besides, what I told you out on the steps still holds true."

"You never show *me* your poetry," Sonia said.

Rue walked to the door where Ralston was still standing. "I'll go out and have a drink with you," he said. "I really want to talk. I'll be back in a few minutes," he added to Sonia.

Ralston could see an explosion forming in Sonia's throat that would more than rival any he had previously witnessed. "No," he said. "I have a dinner engagement. I'm late already. I'll get in touch with you later," he said to a place on the wall halfway between Rue and Sonia, and fairly ran out of the room.

Ralston had dinner, a very large, lengthy dinner, in the first Italian restaurant he came across. He had wine with the meal and brandy with the dessert. Then he went to the phone booth of the nearest drugstore and told Slingbot all (that was relevant) of the conversation. Slingbot was pleased. "It's obviously blackmail," he said. "Simple blackmail. She's trying to hold him up for the money."

"Her story convinced me," Ralston said. "Or almost did," he added, remembering the reservations he had felt.

"She's an accomplished liar," Slingbot said. "You get to be like that when you whore around Europe like she did. I'm having lunch with Jerry Simpson tomorrow. I want you to be there and tell him everything both of them said to you."

"I'm not sure that would help —" Ralston began.

"Just let us decide that," Slingbot said. "All we want is a fair shake for everybody. Did you get a chance to tell her that you're a college professor?"

"Rue knows that I don't know Washington Jones," Ralston said. "I met them both at the same time."

"That's too bad. We'll figure something out. One o'clock then." Slingbot had hung up.

Ralston felt very tired. He had almost a full pint of brandy in his room. He bought a paperback copy of Flaubert's *Temptation of St. Anthony* and read it until he went to sleep.

V

Ralston had left a call for eight. Almost immediately after he got up, he reread the letter from Anne and began typing a letter to her:

Dear Anne,

If I underestimate your aesthetic perceptions, you underestimate my common sense. I have never understood why people always assume that artists do not have common sense merely because they usually reject its dictates. It is very much like assuming that someone does not have a radio simply because he does not buy the products advertised on it. If I could only continue my sales-resistance, my refusal to listen to the annoying voice of the announcer in my skull, I might even become the poet I have dreamed of becoming. I might even, past becoming the poet I have dreamed of becoming, write some good poems.

Certainly San Francisco is neither as good or as bad as I had pictured it. I have met some fools and no angels. The announcer of common sense discloses the cast. But if I could force myself not to listen to him, there is a station underneath trying to get through (like those Mexican stations that make a ghostlike interference to the programs I listen to on my portable radio here) — a mysterious bit of almost unheard music or five words uttered in a strange tongue — and I will not believe that, good or bad, the sounds are merely static. I could not afford to believe it.

You are right in assuming that a series of affairs (I believe you mentioned twelve as a number) would keep me listening to the important words of the idiot announcer. This may be the reason why, with one or two exceptions, I have remained so faithful to you throughout our marriage. Why you have remained faithful to me, since you believe his words important to listen to, I can only think is from inertia or loyalty.

He stopped typing. This was a little strong. He was blaming her (she would think that *she* was the voice of the announcer) for his not rising to the occasion, or rather for not finding any occasion to rise to. And where in the last few days had he heard even a hint of the ghostly voice of the Mexican radio station? With the fish perhaps — and he turned the whole radio off. Since then there had been no hint, except in the rhetoric of his ambition, that the station was not off the air forever.

I exaggerated badly, [he continued] but your letter irritated me when you said that you loved only "plain, simple Jim Ralston" as if my poetry were like robes one puts on for a lodge meeting. The trouble is that I sometimes suspect it is — and this is intolerable.

Don't let my letter spoil your trip. I'm berating you when I should be berating myself. As a matter of fact, I'm writing you because I did not write a poem when I should have.

And of course I love you just as much. And miss you too — physically, emotionally, spiritually. I wish right now, as I write the last paragraph of this letter, that I were back in Boston with you and San Francisco had never been invented by the Indians.

Love,
Jim

He went out and mailed the letter and had breakfast. He felt much better.

The bus he took to Slingbot's was unaccountably fast and he arrived there at ten minutes of one. He rang the buzzer several times but no one appeared and he could not even hear it sounding upstairs.

He tried the door and found that it was open. As he walked up the flight of stairs, he could hear the echoing tones of Slingbot's public voice humming like the sound of a thousand bees. As he got to the door he could distinguish some of the words, "unparalleled fakery that could only fool a professor," "nineteenth-century hooliganism." He knocked. Nothing happened. He knocked again. Slingbot's voice, private this time, answered. "Come on in, God damn it," it said. "Can't you see I'm recording?"

Slingbot was sitting in the red armchair with a sheaf of papers in his lap and what looked like an enormously expensive piece of tape-recording equipment on the table beside him. He was wearing a pink bathrobe. As Ralston entered he snapped off the taperecorder and said, "Hello."

"I hope I didn't spoil your recording," Ralston said. "No one answered the bell."

"That's all right. They edit all the interruptions out at the station." Seeing Ralston's puzzlement, he added, "It's my books broadcast for KARE. It's a highbrow FM station over in San Mateo. I've had the program for the last three years. I tape it here and they play it every Thursday evening. They don't pay me anything but it's good publicity."

Ralston remembered the station vaguely. It had started a year before he left. It had no commercials (being financed by a Ford Foundation grant or something) and ran (while he was there) to string quartets, sopranos singing English sea-chanteys, and panel discussions about local and liberal subjects. "I hope I didn't spoil anything," he repeated.

"Oh, no," Slingbot said. "They edit the tape. Very carefully. I sometimes make off-the-cuff remarks just to keep them on their toes." He switched on the recorder and said, again in a public voice, "And, of course, there was the famous incident a few years ago when the Archbishop of San Francisco was arrested in the men's room of the San Diego Zoo for indecent exposure." He switched the machine off again and grinned. "The engineers have a lot of fun cutting them out."

"What if they miss one?" Ralston asked.

"That only happened once," Slingbot said. "A couple of years ago. It didn't cause too much serious trouble." He straightened the papers in his lap. "I'd better finish the broadcast before Jerry comes in," he said. "I'm in the process of reviewing a new edition of the *Beowulf.*"

Ralston, who had had to struggle through the guttural mysteries of Anglo-Saxon as a graduate student at Columbia, felt mildly curious. "You mean a new translation?"

"A new edition," Slingbot said, clearing his throat — his voice had already become half-public. "Replacing Klaeber's."

"I didn't know that you knew Anglo-Saxon," Ralston said. "Know Anglo-Saxon!" Slingbot's voice had by now become fully public. "I've translated a number of poems in Anglo-Saxon!" He switched on the tape recorder and began reading from the typed manuscript. "So Mr. Grimwald's edition won't be of very great interest to lovers of literature — real literature not schoolbook literature. The fact of the matter is — and it should have been apparent to anyone with half an ear for poetry years ago — that the *Beowulf* is a hoax, an enormous fake. It was mysteriously *discovered* in the Cottonian library in the late eighteenth century at just about the time Chatterton was *discovering* the Rowley poems and Macpherson was *discovering* Ossian. The anonymous gentleman who perpetrated this hoax was more ingenious and more learned than either of those two (although he had to fake a fire in the library to explain the condition of the manuscript) but anyone who bothers to examine the poetic contents of it — who is not a professor or an idiot — will recognize the mixture of pale Christianity and picturesque bedtime-story folktale that is typical of all antiquarian writing in the late eighteenth century. Beowulf is a hero directly out of one of Sir Walter Scott's novels. Even a glance at the energetic and mystical poetry that the Anglo-Saxons really did write will show you the difference. The *Beowulf* is ersatz. It is the Piltdown Man of literature. If scholars like Professor Grimwald were not even stupider than their anthropological counterparts, this hoax would have been exposed long ago." Slingbot gave a wicked grin at Ralston and looked at his watch. "I seem to be running out of time," he said to the vast, invisible, and future audience of KARE. "Next week I'll be back with some more books, if they let me stay on the air after this broadcast." He shut off the recorder. "I always say that," he said to Ralston. "It scares them at the station." He switched the tape recorder on again. "Next week I will also tell you, unless something is done about it pretty quickly, about the persecution of a fine Negro artist in a manner more appropriate to Jackson, Mississippi, than to San Francisco. This is Arthur Slingbot saying good evening." He turned off the recorder and settled back in the armchair. "That was a pretty fine broadcast if I do say so myself."

"What if Sonia hears about it," Ralston objected. "Won't that cause trouble?"

"I want to cause her trouble," Slingbot said. "Two can play the game of blackmail. I want her to know that if she goes on with this plot she's going to have me to fight."

"Does the lawyer know that you've put that remark in your broadcast?" Ralston asked maliciously.

"No. And don't tell him." Slingbot looked worried. "Please don't say anything about it to him. Jerry's very cautious and doesn't like publicity. And he doesn't understand the psychology of people like Sonia like I do." He paused. "What did you think of the *Beowulf* part?"

"It was very interesting," Ralston said. "Do you really believe what you were saying."

Slingbot smiled. "People have to be shaken up," he said. "Besides I've never liked *Beowulf*. I hated it when I had to read it at school." He got up and closed the tape recorder. "I'd better put on some hot water for tea. Madelaine's bringing in some stuff for sandwiches and picking up Jerry. They ought to be here any minute now." He left the room. Ralston picked up a magazine from the coffee table beside his chair and thumbed through it. It contained, as he suspected it would, a poem by Slingbot — a long poem that seemed to be about the hydrogen bomb and St. Augustine. He was stumbling through the second Latin quotation in it when the front door opened and Madelaine appeared, carrying a shopping bag. "Hello, Jim," she said. Ralston stood up. "Jim," she said, moving her head in the direction of the person who was coming in the door behind her, "This is Mr. Simpson. Mr. Simpson, Mr. Ralston."

Gerald Simpson, to Ralston's somewhat uncomfortable surprise, was a small but dignified Negro of about the same age as Slingbot. He was wearing a dark blue business suit. He walked up to Ralston with an extended hand. "Very glad to meet you, Mr. Ralston," he said.

Ralston shook hands with him. He had a Rotarian handshake that reminded Ralston somehow of his own father's. "And I'm glad to meet *you*, Mr. Simpson," he said with equal formality.

"We're going to have bologna," Madelaine said to Ralston. "I hope you like bologna. You two just sit down and talk and

I'll have everything on the table in a minute." She moved purposively toward the kitchen leaving them both standing awkwardly in the middle of the room.

Ralston sat down first. Less than a second later Mr. Simpson followed. There was a long silence. Ralston cleared his throat. Mr. Simpson looked at him closely. "I hear you're a friend of Mr. Jones," he said.

Ralston started to say that Jones was just a casual acquaintance — it was obvious that Slingbot had not told the lawyer the truth — but it suddenly occurred to him that this disclaimer might leave him open to misunderstanding, that Mr. Simpson might feel that he was unwilling merely to call a Negro a friend. The whole thing could be cleared up later. "Yes," he said. "I haven't known him very long though."

"I talked to him today," Mr. Simpson did not seem to be very interested in what he was saying. "Very tall boy. Wonder if he ever played basketball."

"I don't know," Ralston said. "I don't think so." Another silence followed which was only broken by the sound of Madelaine yelling "Lunch is ready" from the dining room. Both of them waited for the other to be the first to walk through the door to the dining room. After a brief, unspoken but violent, contest of wills Ralston won and was able to follow Mr. Simpson into the dining room and be the last to be seated.

Slingbot greeted Mr. Simpson with a casual wave of a hand. "Hi, Jerry," he said. "How's the politician?"

"Things are going remarkably well, Arthur," Mr. Simpson said.

"Jerry's a bigwig in the Democratic Party in his district," Slingbot said to Ralston. "I'm surprised he lets himself associate with a dangerous anarchist like me."

"It is always a pleasure to visit you, Arthur," Mr. Simpson said formally.

The lunch was buffet style and caused a certain amount of confusion. There was bologna (Madelaine, unfortunately, had not been joking), lettuce, mayonnaise, pickles, and sandwich buns. Ralston tried unsuccessfully to hide from Madelaine the fact that he was making his sandwich merely out of lettuce and mayonnaise. "Are you on a diet, Jim?" she asked.

"I'm just not hungry," Ralston said, stifling an urge to tell her exactly what he thought of people who use cellophane-wrapped lunch meats. Anne had been guilty of the same thing, he remembered. It had taken him a full year to break her of the habit.

"Does anyone want mustard?" Slingbot asked. Mr. Simpson nodded gravely. Slingbot went into the pantry to get it.

"Isn't this fun," Madelaine said. "It's just like a picnic." She poured a cup of tea for everybody. Slingbot came back from the pantry with the mustard and sat down.

"I've decided not to take the case," Mr. Simpson said suddenly. "I talked to the boy this morning and I don't like his story."

Slingbot was biting into his sandwich. He hastily swallowed, almost choking in the process. "Now, just a minute," he said.

"The boy," Mr. Simpson went on, undeterred by the interruption, "claims that he cannot remember how he got home, that he was too intoxicated to remember. Do you know how far it is from the party to the place where he lives?"

"I think," Madelaine began, but Mr. Simpson raised a hand to stop her. "Three and one quarter miles. I measured it this morning. Now it is possible to presume that he might have taken a cab, but the boy assured me himself that he didn't have enough money with him to have taken one. None of his friends claim to have driven him home. How did he get there?"

"A bus," Ralston suggested.

"It is relatively impossible, Mr. Ralston, to get from the district where the party was held to Mr. Jones' home by public transportation at that time of night."

"He might have walked," Slingbot said.

"Indeed, he might have walked," Mr. Simpson said. "I do not say that he didn't. All I say is that such a story would not be likely to convince a jury." Mr. Simpson leaned back and placidly took a bite of his sandwich and a sip of his tea.

"Is that all that you're worrying about, Jerry?" Slingbot asked in a half-persuasive, half-angry voice. "Because if it is—"

"It is one of the many factors that deeply disturb me," Mr. Simpson said. "There is another one of equal importance. Perhaps you have not heard of it yet. The gentlemen at the police station say that Mr. Jones had several scratches on his face and hands when he was brought in."

"They beat him up before they brought him in," Slingbot said angrily.

"Naturally that thought occurred to me, too, Arthur," Mr. Simpson said mildly. "But when I saw him this morning I looked at his face and hands very carefully. There are scratches. Long shallow scratches. And the police of this city do not generally wear long fingernails."

"Did you ask him where he got them?" Ralston asked. He had finished his lettuce sandwich and was sipping his tea and enjoying Slingbot's discomfiture.

"I did and he admitted that he did not know where he received the scratches. He suggested that he might have fallen into a bush while he was intoxicated."

"Why not?" Slingbot asked.

"No reason." Mr. Simpson was patient. "That might easily be the explanation for the scratches. But everything in his story is so vague, so filled with mights."

"Can't you tell the truth when you hear it?" Slingbot was now fully angry. "I heard that boy's story and I'd bet everything I have that he's telling the truth."

"The truth, Arthur!" Mr. Simpson raised his brown hand again as a kind of protection — whether against the truth or Slingbot, Ralston could not tell. "The truth may be very important in art and poetry, but the logical is important with the law. And if we stipulate that Mr. Jones is telling the complete truth, what facts do we have to work with? That he does not know where he was between twelve and six in the morning. The prosecution would be glad to concede that. That he is certain that he could not have done such a thing. You and I — and even the prosecution — may believe him when he says this, that he is certain. But what does this prove? Merely that *he* is certain. Even if he is telling the absolute truth in all respects, this does not shake the case against him."

"What about not being able to drive a car?" Ralston asked.

"Ah!" Mr. Simpson turned to Ralston as if seeing him for the first time. "There we have the crux of the matter. If the jury could believe him there. But again there is no possibility of proving anything. Not being able to drive is a negative capability, to use a phrase that I believe your fellow poet Emerson coined. One can prove that one can do something, but it is hard to prove that one cannot do something. Besides, there is no question that Mr. Jones has not driven in cars before and watched their drivers do the simple mechanical operations of driving. If he were in this intoxicated trance — and remember, under the other hypothesis he walked a distance of three and a quarter miles to his house while he was in it — he might easily have driven a car although he had never driven before!"

"Fantastic!" said Slingbot. "Absolutely fantastic!"

"Life often is," said Mr. Simpson. He finished off his sandwich and took another sip of tea. "Tell me," he said, "do you know if the girl, this Miss Liebowitz, has described the manner in which her assailant drove the car?"

"She said he drove erratically," Ralston said, unconsciously lengthening his vocabulary for Mr. Simpson. "She says he kept driving the wrong way."

Mr. Simpson nodded his head.

Slingbot exploded. "Jerry," he said in a booming angry voice that lost every trace of Mr. Pickwick, "do you really mean that you refuse to take the case?"

Mr. Simpson brought out a pipe and began filling it. "I'm afraid I do," he said.

"You have the colossal ego to act as judge and jury before your client is even tried? To wash your hands of him simply because there isn't at the moment an open and shut case in his favor? I suppose you never defended any client who has a weaker story than he does?"

Mr. Simpson was unperturbed. "Many clients. In fact, most. But there is a kind of responsibility one assumes when one volunteers to defend a client without fee."

"If it's a question of money —" Slingbot began, with, Ralston noted, considerably less enthusiasm.

Mr. Simpson looked mildly offended. "I wouldn't have offered my services to begin with if there had been," he said.

"It's a matter of reputation. I've been asked to run for State Assembly for my district next fall. If I seem to be grandstanding on a racial prejudice case that is obviously nothing of the kind, I'll lose more good will among my constituents than I'll gain."

"But there's no question of publicity," Slingbot said. "Every-one wants it settled out of court. All anyone wants is to keep things quiet."

Mr. Simpson smiled a bleak smile. "I hope you won't be offended, Arthur, but I've known you for more than twenty years. Somehow everything you get excited about becomes a public issue."

"You didn't used to be afraid of public issues, Jerry," Slingbot said slowly. "I remember the Turlock Three."

Mr. Simpson looked upset for the first time. "For God's sake, why bring that up!" he said. "It was over twenty years ago."

Slingbot, with a purposeful and rather sadistic look on his face, poured himself another cup of tea. He turned to Ralston. "I don't suppose you ever heard of the Turlock Three," he said. "It happened over twenty years ago like Jerry told you. Three Mexican farm laborers got drunk one night and raped a white girl. They left her out in the field where they had raped her. It was a cold night and she died of pneumonia in the hospital two days later. The woman was something of a tramp herself and the boys were headed for what at most would have been a twenty-year sentence. Then the Communist Party got interested in the case. They formed a Defense Committee For The Turlock Three. Jerry here was vice-chairman."

"You know as well as I do, Arthur," Mr. Simpson said, "that the Committee wasn't all Communist. There were some very respectable people on it."

"They got the boys hanged," Slingbot went on inexorably. "Managed to get enough publicity to get the boys hanged."

"That was a very long time ago, Arthur," Mr. Simpson said in some sorrow. "And you were part of the Committee too."

"Now Jerry here," Slingbot went on to Ralston ignoring Mr. Simpson's objection, "is a very respectable registered Democrat. He doesn't like public issues. He gave them up years ago."

"That just isn't fair, Arthur —" Mr. Simpson began.

"As I was saying on my radio program just the other day, it is the special responsibility of ex-Communists, or ex-fellow-travelers," he added as Mr. Simpson opened his mouth to object, "to make up for things a bit by standing by the causes they once helped to ruin." His voice cracked like a whip. "Don't you agree, Jerry?"

The whip cut Mr. Simpson, but he did not bleed. "It's an interesting generalization," he said.

"Besides," Slingbot went on, his eyes gleaming, "I have already told everyone that you would take the case. I would have to explain. Publicly explain."

Mr Simpson capitulated. "Well —" he said.

Slingbot then, rather as if he were adding honey to a dose of castor oil, said pleasantly, "Besides, we now have some new information. The girl is attempting to blackmail Jones. Tell him about your conversation with her, Jim."

Ralston, lost in admiration of Slingbot's own blackmailing technique, could hardly begin. He finally did manage to tell the story, being somewhat impeded by Slingbot's interruptions ("You see. It's a squeeze play. She pretends she doesn't want to negotiate and has Rue Talcott to do all the bidding for her") and by Madelaine, whose questions, detailed and specific, involved whether and under what conditions Rue and Sonia were living together.

At the end of the recital Mr. Simpson folded his hands. "It sounds more hopeful," he said. "At the moment I feel inclined to take the case. The girl does not sound as if she would make an effective witness. And the offer of settlement does have some elements of coercion in it." He looked at Slingbot. "But if I do take the case, I must have a great many more facts. Someone must have seen the boy leave the party and have noticed the time. Someone must have observed and be willing to testify exactly how intoxicated this Miss Liebowitz was. Someone may even have seen her on the sidewalk when she was picked up by this car."

"Yes." Slingbot was mild and enthusiastic now. "You'll have to check into all that."

"The point is," Mr. Simpson continued, slowly and with great emphasis, "that even if I had the time to do all the necessary investigation myself, which I do not, I would be very awkward at it. These people simply aren't in my milieu. I do not understand why people go to drunken parties or write poetry. I never have."

"That's fair enough, Jerry," Slingbot said. "You shouldn't have to do all the work. I'm going to be tied up for the next couple of days, but after that I'll be glad to do most of the investigating myself."

"I'm afraid that two days will not be soon enough," Mr. Simpson said. "In two days the witnesses will have entirely different stories to tell. They will have heard what happened and will be tempted to embroider their account of what they saw and heard. Witnesses don't mean to be dishonest, but give them two or three days to think about their story and they always are." He looked sadly at Slingbot, Ralston, and Madelaine. "It will have to be done now. Immediately."

"I'm sorry," Slingbot said, making himself another sandwich now that everything was practically settled. "It's impossible. I have to rehearse all the rest of today and tomorrow, maybe through Thursday. I'm recording my poetry for Fantasy Records — with Shorty Fitzgerald's combo behind it."

"Poetry and jazz!" Ralston exclaimed with some malice. "Rexroth and Patchen and now you."

"It's not such a new thing," Slingbot said. "People have been experimenting with it for a long time. As a matter of fact, I may have been the first that ever tried it — except for the French, of course. Way back in the late twenties. I read some poems in an after-hours joint in Pittsburgh and Bix Biederbecke improvised behind them. Rexroth talks as if the idea is new, but it's been going on for years. I remember once in Berlin —"

"Couldn't we —" Madelaine started to interrupt, but Slingbot said, "No, my dear. I won't be able to find any time at all. This sort of thing takes time. The trouble with all the poetry and jazz records that I've heard is that they don't rehearse. The poet just reads and the musicians blow. Shorty and I have decided to work until my voice is just as much a part of the combo as a horn or a saxophone."

"I was about to suggest," Madelaine said shortly, "couldn't Jim and I do all the interviewing?" She turned to Ralston. "It would be fun, wouldn't it?"

"I'm afraid I haven't been much of a success at interviewing witnesses so far," Ralston said. "People like Sonia rather baffle me."

"They won't all be like Sonia," Madelaine said. "Come on. We'll take the car and finish it all this afternoon."

Slingbot's silence did not indicate much enthusiasm for the project. This tempted Ralston. "If you all think it would be a good idea," he said.

Slingbot finished his second sandwich. He belched slightly. "I'm afraid I'll have to use the car to get to rehearsal," he said.

"Nonsense," Madelaine smiled in the way she always did when she was going to, had to, win the argument. "You told me that the rehearsal is down on Fillmore Street. You can take the bus directly there. Or we could drive you."

"Exactly who are we going to interview?" Ralston asked, cooperating with Madelaine by changing the subject before Slingbot could think of a new reason for objecting.

"I would suggest," said Mr. Simpson, also possibly cooperating out of a malice of his own, "that you see the host of the party first. He would know, or one hopes that he would know, most of the guests that he invited."

"Bobbie Sherrel gave the party," Slingbot said. "You'll do well to get any sort of coherent statement out of him."

"He'll at least know who was drunk and who wasn't," Madelaine said. "That's all he talks about except religion." She turned to Ralston. "You'll like Bobbie. He's a dear."

"You'd better get the car back in time to shop for dinner," Slingbot said, somewhat ungraciously accepting the inevitable. "There is nothing in the house to eat."

"Oh, I can't promise that," Madelaine said. "We may run into some important clues. Or someone may hit Jim over the head and steal the Maltese Falcon and I'll have to rescue it."

"Have the car back by five," Slingbot repeated.

Madelaine drove and let an unenthusiastic Mr. Simpson and an annoyed Slingbot off at their respective destinations. Before Mr. Simpson left them he said to Ralston, "Be sure to make anyone you get information from repeat his story to you several times. Let him get it fixed in his mind so he won't change it. I don't care what story they tell, but I want to be sure they tell the same story on the witness stand."

"And don't talk to her friends," Slingbot told him as he left them. "There may be others in the plot besides Rue."

As they drove together to Bobbie Sherrel's house (it was located in that no man's land of ugly houses that is neither in the Negro district or in the Tenderloin but seems somehow to be part of both), Madelaine was in good spirits. "My, Arthur was angry," she said. "I don't think he trusts me with you."

Ralston refused to rise to the bait. "Do you plan to visit everybody that went to the party?" he asked.

"Oh, we couldn't. There were probably almost fifty people there and Bobbie won't know the names of more than a third of them. We'll just pick up clues." She laughed. "Why were you so nice about coming along? I expected you to object more than Arthur."

"I've learned to accept the inevitable," Ralston said. "Everyone seems to want to drag me into something. I'll just let them."

"Do you think I'm trying to drag you into something?"

"Yes," Ralston said firmly. "Is the house far from here? Let's stop and have a drink before we go in." And he could get some peanuts at the bar. He was hungry after that lettuce sandwich.

"We're only a block away," Madelaine said. "And Bobbie usually has something to drink at his house." She stared at him speculatively. "You know, Jim, I wonder if you're becoming an alcoholic."

"It's just San Francisco," Ralston said. "I'm very calm in Boston." They were silent until Madelaine parked the car.

Bobbie Sherrel lived in an apartment built on the top of a garage which was in back of a very large rooming house that had once been a mansion. The stairs leading up to it were iron. His doorknocker, Ralston stared at before he recognized what it was, was a large carved crucifix of black wood attached to a chain. He hesitated at the threshold. "Good God," he said to Madelaine.

"I know," she said. "It always makes people nervous. Bobbie's very religious." She banged the cross against the door itself. It made a faintly booming sound.

In a moment the door opened. A man of about twenty-seven wearing paint-splotched blue jeans and a T-shirt, with a red beard and moustache, and, what Ralston had never seen before, long red eyelashes, answered the door. "Come on in, Madelaine," he said. "I'm painting, but I suppose I can spare a few minutes."

"Bobbie, this is Jim Ralston," Madelaine said. They shook hands. By now it seemed appropriate. "Come in, come in," Bobbie Sherrel repeated. "But be careful of the painting on the floor."

The painting on the floor indeed almost blocked their entrance. It was an enormous canvas — almost ten feet by five feet. Ralston edged around it. It consisted of a two-foot bluish spot thick with pigment surrounded on all sides by an almost equally thick bluish-green surface. As he looked at it Ralston blinked his eyes. The painting literally sparkled.

Bobbie Sherrel was watching his reaction. He laughed a deep bronchial laugh that was somewhat out of keeping with his pixyish body. "Carborundum, that's the secret, carborundum. I buy it at machine shop." He went to the workbench and took a handful of fine black powder from a coffee can and sprinkled it at random on the painting. New sparkles appeared. "It lasts forever," he said. He turned to Madelaine. "I call this one 'Love Exploding Through The Universe At The Coronation Of The Blessed Virgin Mary.'"

"Oh," Madelaine said. "Is there some place where we can sit down?"

"I'm afraid not," Bobbie said. "I took all the chairs out of the house when I gave the party. Did you know that I gave a party?"

"That's what we came to talk to you about," Madelaine said.

Bobbie looked bewildered. "Oh, really! You weren't there too, were you? I don't remember what happened very clearly." He paused and then his face cleared. "We could all go into the bedroom and sit on the bed," he said.

They walked through the long studio room, cluttered with all kinds of painting equipment, unused easels, stacked paintings, even two saw-horses, into a relatively neat and compact bedroom. The bed, which was merely an outsized mattress placed in the middle of the floor, was not made. The room was dominated by a huge collage which consisted of a cheap lithograph of the Sacred Heart of Jesus entirely surrounded by illustrations clipped from truss advertisements. There was an orange crate serving as a table by the bed. On it was a Missal and a Breviary. On the wall behind the makeshift table was another crucifix.

Bobbie made an effort to straighten the bedcovers. "Sit down," he said. "There's a half gallon of wine left over from the party in the corner. I'll get some glasses. I haven't wanted to try it by myself because I was afraid somebody pissed in it." He saw a look of horror on Ralston's face and he quickly added, "I don't mean they really did. I'm sure they didn't. But they're always doing things like that at my parties." He took three glasses from a stack of nine or ten in another corner of the room and poured a great deal of wine into each. He drank a sip of wine from his own before handing theirs to Madelaine and Ralston. "See," he said. "The wine is perfectly all right."

"You really haven't heard about the business about Sonia?" Madelaine asked. She took a little sip of the wine as did Ralston. It was very sour but seemingly untainted.

"Sonia?" Bobbie asked. "Was Sonia at the party? You know, I rather thought she must have been. There were a number of wine stains on the wall in the morning and one of my paintings was stepped on."

Madelaine took another sip of the wine and gave a surprisingly accurate summary of what happened and what was said to have happened. It occurred to Ralston for the first time that she was taking, if not the cause, the investigation quite seriously.

Bobbie pulled at his red beard and took a large swallow of wine. "I certainly can't tell you when Judge left," he said. "I was sure he was here in the morning when we all woke up and had scrambled eggs. I know Rue and Greg Taxon were. And I don't even remember Sonia being at the party at all."

Ralston, spurred on by the look of disappointment on Madelaine's face, took a hand in the investigation. "Was there any other Negro besides Jones at the party?" he asked. "Someone Sonia might have confused him with?"

"There were quite a few Negroes," Bobbie Sherrel said. "There are always quite a few Negroes," he added, as if the thought had just occurred to him.

"But were there any as tall as Washington Jones, any that looked like him?"

"There was one that I was arguing theology with," Bobbie said. "He told me that he subscribed to the *Catholic Worker*. I remember he was Negro because I accused him of sounding like an Irish Catholic."

"He doesn't sound like the type we're looking for," Ralston said.

"I don't know." Bobbie, having contributed a suspect, was concerned to protect his status. "He seemed violent. And I believe he did leave the party at around four in the morning. Very much like Jones. I remember noticing the resemblance. Of course, it might have been Jones himself I was talking with. I was very drunk at the time."

"Then you don't know his name?" Madelaine asked.

"No. I don't remember his name or anyone else he talked to. But he must have talked to some other people. Unless he *was* Jones."

"Who would have been sober enough to remember?"

"If I had been sober enough to know that, *I* would have been sober enough to remember," Bobbie told her reasonably. "Rue might or Bill Benson might. I don't think Ryan would. And Grace was with Eddie Bowen —"

Ralston, who felt sure that Bobbie was capable of going on dreamily listing names and half-names all afternoon, interrupted him. "One of the things that we came over to get from you," he said, "is a list of names of the people at the party that you can remember being there about that time."

"I don't think that would be much help to you," Bobbie said. "The ones I'm really certain of Madelaine would know already. They all know each other. But I do have an idea. Do you have a car with you?"

"Yes," Madelaine said, somewhat unenthusiastically.

Bobbie looked at the drawn blinds of the bedroom. "Is it sunny outside?" he asked.

"No," Madelaine said firmly. "It's very cloudy."

"Then they'll all be at The Birdcage," Bobbie said. "Otherwise they'd be at Aquatic Park. We can drive down to The Birdcage and talk to everybody. Somebody there will know what happened. I haven't been out of this house for two days anyway. I need a break."

"That's not a bad idea," Madelaine said. "Are you sure they'll be down there?"

"All but a few. It will give you a start anyway. Of course, that won't help with the unknown people. What I really should do is give another party and all the same people I don't know would come and you could ask *them* questions."

Ralston put his wine glass down. He was glad not only of the chance to put it down but of the prospect of getting something drinkable to replace it. "I don't imagine another party will be necessary," he said. "Someone at The Birdcage will know something. Let's go right now."

Madelaine, however, was off on another track. "A party for all the witnesses," she said. "That might be just the thing that would clear this up. Not at your house but ours."

"You've been reading too many detective stories," Ralston said. "I can just imagine how Mr. Simpson would love that idea."

Madelaine got up from the bed and put on her coat. "Well, I can ask Arthur about it later," she said. Ralston and Bobbie Sherrel also arose, Ralston taking this opportunity for a more close examination of the collage of the Sacred Heart and truss illustrations on the wall. It was very odd, but there was a force behind it. Bobbie was watching him. "I'm glad you didn't laugh," he said wistfully. "I call it 'Homage to St. Teresa.' Sometimes I think that she's the only one of the saints that would have really understood my painting."

VI

"Loneliness is the essential characteristic of Alice," Ralston was saying. "She wanders through both of her books, the rabbit hole and the chessboard, and never meets one person, one creature that wants to do anything more than surprise her." He looked around at the group he was sitting with at the bar. They looked back at him. "Only once, when she and the faun are lost in the forest that makes them forget their names, does she find any vestige of companionship. And it is the most anonymous kind of companionship —"

"Looking glass food isn't good for you," Rue said, filling his glass from the pitcher of beer kindly provided by the new guest at the table. "And looking glass people can't be friendly to non-looking glass people. It's like cowboys and Indians only metaphysical."

"The metaphysics work both ways," Ralston said. "Cowboys are pretty stupid creatures without Indians and Indians without cowboys only have the vast prairie lands of their own imaginations. Imagine," he said, pouring some of the beer into Madelaine's glass (who was frankly bored and waiting for Ralston to stop talking and for Rue to go away so she could ask the rest of the people some questions about the party. "It has been almost two hours that we have been here," her face clearly said. "And we have spent an hour and forty-five minutes of it watching you get drunk and talk art with that ridiculous boy."). "Imagine what a boring child Alice must have been on her own side of the looking glass and how equally boring the carefully ordered world of the looking glass and the rabbit hole must have been without Alice!"

"I think Alice was a pathological liar," Madelaine said. "She lied about everything that happened to her. Most children do." She stared hard at Gregory Taxon as she said this. He knew something about what had happened to Judge that evening that he didn't want to tell her. She was sure of this. If all these idiots would go away she would squeeze that information out of his baby face (if that made him sound like a pimple she couldn't help it) in two minutes. He definitely hesitated when she asked him. Jim must have noticed him hesitate too. *He* was a great help — getting drunk on all that awful ale and showing off to Rue Talcott and inviting all these people who weren't even at the party over to the table when they could have been getting everything settled. She noticed that he was speaking to her "— the logical ending of the dream."

"What?" she said.

"I said that the only thing that Alice ever lied about was the logical ending of the dream."

"Oh," she said.

The new guest, Dr. McCreedy, who until ten minutes ago had been a drunken Irishman at the end of the bar singing to himself and sending them free but unwelcome, to Madelaine at least, pitchers of beer, but who had turned out, when he had sat down even more unwelcomely at their table, to be besides a drunken Irishman a Jungian analyst with a real M.D., if you could believe him, named Stephen McCreedy, now joined abruptly into the conversation. "Man first discovers isolation in childhood," he said. "Alice mirrors this discovery. No pun intended." He beamed at the rest of the table.

"But it's beyond childhood in Alice," Ralston began. "That's the whole point of it —"

"No, my friend." The Irishman banged his huge fist on the table. "The loneliness of childhood. That's the point of it. The loneliness of childhood where you find out for the first time that chairs and butterflies and adults can't really talk to you." He hiccupped slightly. "The imago is a butterfly," he said.

Madelaine let her mind wander. It was not that conversations like this bored her but that she had heard so many of them — using a book or a play or even a movie to dig with at the roots of big meanings. And she had never seen any of them change anybody's behavior or make anybody wiser or safer or happier. She wondered whether, if the world were entirely made up of women, there would be such conversations. She had heard women engage in them, had even herself participated in them, when there was not a man present, but it was always as if, to her at least, they were expecting a group of men to come in and finish the conversation, finally talking to silence, these imaginary men, the women who had started it.

"In an absolutely literal sense the child is father to the man," Ralston was saying. "He is as important and as traumatic and as hard to remember as one's real father. He is an authority figure to all of us — not merely to someone that worshipped him so obviously as Lewis Carroll or Edward Lear did, but also to those that hated him like Freud and Joyce. The father may bother us for the few years when the Oedipus complex is important, but the child will sit in judgment on us for the rest of our lives —"

Madelaine took another swallow of unwelcome beer and let her thoughts drift again. She wondered what sort of conversations Jim had with that psychiatrist wife of his. Whether they — It was a very warm afternoon. She noticed that the back of Dr. McCreedy's hands were covered with red hair. Even though he was almost bald. He was too heavy. But he must have been a handsome man twenty years ago. And a psychiatrist then too. He must really be a psychiatrist because no drunken Irishman was going to tell you that he was a Jungian analyst if he wasn't one. Besides that Jim must believe that he was one because he was showing off to him almost as shamelessly as he was showing off to Rue Talcott and he was married to one. But the red hair on the back of his hands —

"— That's why the Christ Child is so important," Bobbie Sherrel who, after all, had a red beard and a red moustache and red eyelashes was saying. "Imagine God dying on a cross remembering that as a human child, a Christ Child, he had wanted to talk to rabbits and go through mirrors."

"The cross of time," Dr. McCreedy said. "The great serpent. Waiter, bring another pitcher of beer for the table!"

He must be at least fifty, Madelaine thought. I wonder if he's a fairy. He's bought all that beer for everyone and has hardly looked at me the entire time. He's probably after Bobbie. It must be hell for people like that when they get old. Even if they are analysts.

"— I wonder who the patron saint of snark hunting is," Rue was saying.

"Saint Ahab," Ralston said. Madelaine could see that he was particularly pleased with himself. "Send a boy to do a man's job. Saint Ahab who was martyred in the quest for the ultimate boojum."

"Seriously though," Rue said. He was in his element, Madelaine thought. They all were, damn them. "Seriously though, if they had sent a boy to do a man's job, if they had sent children like Rimbaud or Alice snark-hunting or whale-searching, there would have been no danger and they might have finished the job."

This was more interesting. It was, if only in a rather rarefied way, about people. "Do you mean because children are so selfish?" she asked. "Because they're so single-minded?"

"Because they don't believe in patterns," Rue said. Everybody looked at him not understanding his remark any better than Madelaine did but expecting, as Madelaine did not, that there was something in the remark to understand.

"I think I understand what you mean," Ralston was inevitably the one to say. "The adults who went snark-hunting only had the names of their professions — the Bowman, the Baker, the Banker —"

"The Badger," Madelaine muttered.

"They had been patterned and were expecting sequence. And Captain Ahab was *Captain* Ahab."

"But didn't Alice expect sequence too?" Madelaine asked sweetly. She would give him the Badger.

"Yes, but she wasn't alarmed when she didn't get it. She was used to isolation and disorder. Children would make great explorers."

"It isn't just their ability to survive, it's their not seeing in patterns, not being used to things," Rue said. "If an adult gets close to a thing he can't be used to, he collapses."

"Like God," Bobbie Sherrel said. Everybody now looked at Bobbie. "I mean, isn't that what Moby Dick and the Boojum are supposed to be? I haven't read either of the books but I thought they were from what you were saying."

And they were on the paper chase again, pursuing a meaningless three-letter word around and outside the universe. Madelaine herself thought she would back Alice against the crew of the Pequod any day — but not because she was a *child*. Alice was a woman and women do not go on useless journeys. Not at least, she thought to herself ruefully, intentionally.

She began, for it was a very hot day indeed and she was bored, forming in her mind what she would say to them if they, these males, if they had asked *her* about Alice. It was obvious, she would say. *Alice* never had any intention of hunting Jabberwocks. She engaged in no ridiculous quests. In Wonderland Alice takes no side trips — or at least none that are not at least concerned with getting her out of the rabbit hole and in the Looking Glass her only concern is to get to the end of the chessboard by the straightest route possible. And it is the ungainly male creatures in the book, the indirectly moving knights and the sleepy kings, that get in her way.

Ralston, with a sidewise lurch that did remind her of a chessboard knight, was getting up from the table. He would not take beer from the pitcher but insisted on going up to the bar and buying ale after silly ale. And keeping the conversation abstract and away from the party. And he would expect her to stay here patiently the whole afternoon. And to be driven to his hotel room if, indeed, he didn't make a pass at her on the way.

And was it, quite frankly, to make precisely this happen that she had been so unexpectedly enthusiastic about the investigation? She doubted it but was not, she seldom was, certain. Being faithful to Arthur, faithful even in the extent of her flirtations, was a grand gesture — a game like buying groceries (she must phone Arthur and tell him that they will be late with the car), like taking care of children. She did not feel trapped (people were always asking her if she felt trapped, Jim was almost certain to ask her that in the car on the way to the hotel or, at least, on their very next meeting) and she suspected that if this was so at her age (she must even be a year older than Jim) that she would never feel trapped, never feel that she was a prisoner to Arthur, the children, and the grocery lists. And it would only be the feeling of being trapped (for did Alice or any other child feel trapped in the rabbit hole or the looking glass — she should have asked them *that* before they got off on whales) for it was only the feeling of being trapped that could ever force her to be unfaithful.

But why then, she asked herself, am I so concerned with this ridiculous business of running around after clues? Arthur and Jim must both think they have the answer, but if I know, as I do know, that I'm not even trying to be unfaithful, that this is no excuse to be alone with Jim (who is rather a bore and looks *much* older) why on earth am I running around the city (of course, what I'm doing now is not exactly running) why on earth am I running around the city to prove that a Negro I do not particularly like did not beat up a girl that I despise?

She took a long sip of beer. She did not usually allow herself the luxury of questions like that, questions whose answers could merely disturb or rob enjoyment from the game of living exactly the way she lived. ("Almost as if," Madelaine said to herself, "in the middle of a chess game you ask yourself why a knight moves in exactly the way it moves or why the King of Clubs should be higher than the Queen of Clubs") but if she could not allow herself to ask such questions when she wanted to, she would feel trapped and then she would sleep with Ralston.

Besides that, it was all so simple, she thought to herself as she listened with half an ear to the conversation which had now turned to anima and animus in Dostoyevsky. Arthur's world, like the world of this conversation, was so indefinite, was never puzzling because of course there never were, as she supposed there shouldn't be, any right or wrong answers to the puzzle. *She* preferred novels with only one murderer, searches that were demonstrably successful or unsuccessful, things that stayed put while she looked after them. And grocery lists were a bit *too* simple. No, it was clear. The problem of whether or not Washington Jones did or did not attack Sonia Liebowitz in a car at 4:00 AM Sunday morning was complex, difficult, but solvable. It was, she supposed, a different type of intellectual challenge than a metaphysical exegesis of *Alice in Wonderland*, but it was at least fully as meaningful. She felt better. That was it.

In her relief she smiled at Ralston. Smiled so loudly that Ralston who was in the middle of a sentence and not really looking at her stopped speaking and stared. "I'm sorry, Jim," she said. "I was just thinking of something."

Men, of course, didn't have to feel trapped to want to sleep with other women, but she wondered if he did feel trapped. Madelaine knew that he wanted to sleep with her (even, she thought, if he didn't know it yet himself) but what if they had both been in Boston instead of San Francisco? Would he want to then? What would he be like if he were not on vacation? Would he avoid her and other women that were not psychiatrists and faculty wives? But here she was thinking of *that* again and not about the problem, her problem. She was almost as bad as the rest of them. She smiled at Ralston again, a less noisy smile.

Madelaine's first smile had interrupted Ralston's conversation and made him feel guilty. Her second one stopped him altogether and he lapsed into moody silence. They had been talking about heroes and Ralston had taken, against Rue on the one hand and Dr. McCreedy on the other, the, to him, immensely interesting position that children could not be heroes. "Things would be too easy if they could," he had said. "A hero is an adult who is forced by circumstances to behave like a child."

This was the point when Madelaine's first smile happened to happen.

He was, however, able to go on. "Look at Odysseus," he said. "A settled noble who is conscripted into going back to his childhood. There would have been nothing heroic about him if he had been already there. Imagine Alice having the same adventures. If she had been confronted by a Cyclops or turned into a pig by Circe she would look for and find a magic bottle saying "Drink Me."

"Is heroism merely a matter of difficulty?" Dr. McCreedy asked, seemingly subdued into sobriety by the conversation. "Isn't it also a matter of accomplishment? Is a four-minute mile any faster because it is run by a cripple?"

"Adventures of the spirit are not like a four-minute mile," Ralston said, now embarrassingly conscious of the fact that he was, in a way, defending himself. "The impact of an adult mind being forced into the responsibilities of childhood can create something that exists in neither the child's nor the adult's world. Something nearer ultimate reality."

"I don't see that Don Quixote was nearer to ultimate reality than Rimbaud was," Rue said. This was the second time that Madelaine happened to smile.

The ale settled on Ralston's ego like a green stinging jellyfish. He could taste it in his throat and throughout his

mouth. Even Madelaine could understand and laugh at the
appropriateness of Rue's remark. Don Quixote was what he
was to these people and even if he did have a built-in Sancho
Panza in his skull, which was speaking now, that merely made
him the more ridiculous. The poems he hadn't written while
he was here were not written because they could not be written. A trip to the past would be a better place to find them
than a trip to San Francisco. His narrow competent poetry and
his narrow competent wife and his narrow competent job were
waiting for him back in Boston. He was not even a complete
Don Quixote. He was a Don Quixote on vacation.

Even the conversation went along without him. Gregory
Taxon and the Doctor and Bobbie Sherrel were all discussing
jazz and if Rue was silent it was not because he was regretting
the lack of truth in his remark but its painful accuracy. And
Madelaine with her games of love and detection, she was
silent and waiting for him to come to her afterwards, tail
between his legs and windmills forgotten, to be comforted and
teased and petted until the both of them became tired of the
only game they could play together. He suddenly remembered
that in both college and high school he had never actually
played football.

Rue broke in across the chain of conversation. "Have you
read my poetry yet?" he asked. Ralston looked around at
Madelaine expecting to see her smile for the third time but
she was no longer there. She was, he noticed, standing at the
far end of the bar on the way to the lavatories talking animat-
edly to Gregory Taxon. "The poetry I gave you. Have you read
it?" Rue repeated.

"No. Not yet." Ralston, pulled together, was all the person
he would have been in Boston. "I'm on vacation, you know." He
had managed, he noticed from Rue's expression and his silence, by his words and manner to hurt the boy as deeply if
not as accurately as he had hurt him. "I'll get around to it," he
added with no intention of making things better or worse.

The conversation, as unaffected by this byplay as a moving
stream would be by a stick thrown into it, went on its way.
Ralston went to the bar to get another ale. Madelaine, he
noticed, was using the telephone.

When he got back to the table he quietly poured his ale and pretended to listen to what the others were saying. He knew his moods and he knew that even if he had discovered an unpleasant truth about himself, and he suspected he had, the truth would neither be as unpleasant or apparent when the depression went away.

"I didn't mean to put you down," Rue said to him suddenly, again moving like a piece of wood against the stream of conversation that was going on. His voice was almost apologetic. "It's just that heroism doesn't seem to be much of an advantage. You know what I mean."

"Yes, I know what you mean," Ralston said, somewhat mollified by both the apology and the new ale, "but I would hate it to be true and it isn't true. Of course —"

But Madelaine was standing over his shoulder and interrupting him just when he was about to say something really important. "Jim, we've got to go," she was saying. "I've just called Arthur. He's furious. We've got to bring the car back."

It was five o'clock and Arthur must be, as Madelaine must long ago have planned it, furious. Ralston thought for a moment of saying that he for one did not want to leave and that she could very well return to the car to Arthur without his help. He had an ale and a conversation to finish, both more important and less depressing than they had been a few minutes before.

"I —" he began.

"Come on, Jim," Madelaine said in a voice that seemed to him more demanding than the occasion warranted. "We have to go."

It would mean a scene, he saw, if he resisted her. Besides he could always explain things to her on the sidewalk and come back with far less embarrassment in the process. He got up after finishing the swallow of ale, smiled at everybody, and followed Madelaine out of the door.

"For God's sake," Madelaine said as soon as they were out on the sidewalk, "I thought you were going to stay there arguing with me forever. Didn't you see me wink?"

Ralston had not.

"Well I did. I didn't want to have to shout about it at the table but I've discovered where Judge went that night. He was in Sausalito."

"What?"

"In Sausalito. Didn't you notice how nervous Gregory Taxon looked when I asked everybody if they had any idea where Judge had been?"

Ralston had not.

"Well he did. So I caught him the first time he had to go to the men's room. Blocked his way standing there and asking him what he really knew about it. It always works."

"What always works?"

"Asking men questions when they have to urinate — especially after a lot of beer. They lose their dignity and have to tell the truth. Anyway Greg said that Judge phoned him at the party from Sausalito at about two in the morning."

"Why on earth was he making a secret of it?" Ralston asked.

"He wasn't sure that it wouldn't get Judge into trouble. Greg's not very bright."

"Is he certain that it was Jones that called him?"

"Let's start walking toward the car," Madelaine said to him impatiently. "I don't want Rue finding out about this and telling Sonia." They walked briskly, a little too briskly for comfort as the car was parked on a hill. Madelaine, however, was not out of breath. "It was Judge all right," she said. "All we have to do now is to find out how he got back from Sausalito. I did call Arthur. He was furious about having to fix dinner for himself but he finally agreed that we ought to check on this as quickly as possible."

They had reached the car. Madelaine slipped efficiently into the driver's seat and opened the other door for Ralston. Ralston settled back in the seat, a little muzzy from the ale and the mystery. "But what on earth was he doing in Sausalito?" he asked. "And why didn't he remember?"

"That part isn't clear," Madelaine said. She put the car in gear and started to turn around on the hill. "Judge was evidently very drunk. He wanted Greg to borrow a car and take him back to the party."

"I don't see how that helps," Ralston said petulantly. He would, as a matter of fact, rather enjoy a late afternoon ride across the bay to Sausalito, but he did not enjoy being ordered around, almost kidnapped, by Madelaine.

"We're two hours closer to finding out what really happened," Madelaine said. "There obviously aren't very many public places in Sausalito that one can telephone from at two in the morning. We'll check them all and see if we can't pick up his trail."

"How do you know he wasn't calling from somebody's house?"

"Greg said that it sounded like he was in a bar. Lots of noise in the background. And if he had been in somebody's house, he'd have stayed there."

This seemed a bit uncertain in its reasoning to Ralston but he went on to another point. "Why do you think anybody will remember seeing him?"

Madelaine laughed. "People notice Judge when he's drunk. They can't help it. He breaks windows and things."

"Then all we have to do is find a bar with a broken window," Ralston said sarcastically. They were on the Golden Gate Bridge approach and he felt drowsy. "Just a minute," he went on, as the implication finally caught up with him. "I thought Washington Jones was supposed to be as meek as a dove at all times. I thought that was why everybody was so sure that he didn't beat up Sonia."

"I wish you'd call him Judge like everyone else does. Washington Jones sounds so silly. Besides, he isn't violent. He just breaks windows."

They had reached the bridge. Madelaine rather uncharacteristically drove so that the window on her side was next to the toll booth and had a quarter in her hand as she passed through. She looked thoughtful. "I'll admit that what we find out may not make things look better for him," she said. "But at least we may find out what really happened. And Sonia's bound to hear about the phone call and send someone over to investigate if we don't."

The suspension columns of the bridge were a different color than Ralston remembered. They were a funny orange red, a color that somehow looked as if it didn't exist in reality, as if it had been invented for the occasion. He looked at the bay and the Gate in the late afternoon sunshine. Out to the west where there were, in the conceivable distance, Hawaii and China and so much ocean that the mind wearied immediately at the conception of the thought. Never had he had that feeling during the years that he had looked at the Atlantic, although he had once or twice tried to summon it up artificially by quoting distances to himself. It had been no use. The Atlantic was an ocean with Europe on the other side of it — larger and rougher than, say, Lake Erie, but not much different. And this was the Pacific. You could really believe that it spread out forever.

"It's beautiful, isn't it," Madelaine said, for once sensing his mood. "I've always wondered how it would look to someone returning to it."

"Revisiting it," Ralston corrected. "It looks fine. A little too much like a harbor at the end of the world. A little too much of a wall out there maybe."

They were silent all the rest of the way to Sausalito. Madelaine parked the car on the main street of the town. "Where are we going first?" Ralston asked.

"It will be either a bar or an all-night restaurant he called from," Madelaine said. "Greg thinks the call came a little after two but he might be a few minutes wrong. We'll try the bars first."

"All the bars in town?"

"There aren't that many and besides there are only a couple that are likely. I think we'll try the Sea Horse first. It's only a block or so away from here."

Sausalito, Ralston realized as he walked down the street with Madelaine, had changed a great deal in the ten years since he had seen it. Then it had been a spoiled fishing village quainted up into being a resort town on the order, but not on the scale, of Provincetown or Carmel. It had had, or had seemed to have, a soiled dignity and stubborn resistance to major change. Now it had surrendered to the inevitable. It was as if some town on Cape Cod were suddenly discovered to be in fifteen minutes commuting distance from Manhattan. A Suburbia, even if it seemed to be a Suburbia with more FM receivers than television sets, had overwhelmed both the fishermen and the gift shops. The banks all looked as if they had been designed by Frank Lloyd Wright, the drug stores as if they had been imported from Southern California. There were many dogs on the street — although this might also have been true, Ralston could not quite remember, of the second or gift shop layer of the town's archeology. Only the many piers, the bar they were walking towards now was on the edge of one of them, and the bay itself suggested the fishing village, the Ur-Sausalito which, as far as Ralston know, might never have really existed.

"It's changed," he said to Madelaine. "Things have over-flowed into it."

"I suppose it has," Madelaine said. "Arthur and I almost bought a house here when my grandmother died and left me some money, but we finally decided against it. Actually Arthur did. He said that it would depress him, that it would be like living in a bathtub. He's awfully finicky about the way people live."

A dog that looked very much like a large dachshund but which was, as much to its own surprise as anyone else's Ralston felt, purple in color, came out of an alley and sniffed at them. "It is nasty," Madelaine said. "But from the hills there's a beautiful view."

They had arrived at the Sea Horse. It was, as most of the bars in the town were still, a second layer job in architecture. The facade facing the street was constructed of a substance chemically prepared to resemble driftwood and on each side of the door were two wooden mermaids which had been, or were specially constructed to have been, the figureheads of old ships.

The people in the bar were definitely of the latest layer. In it were deposited, from offices in San Francisco which had closed at four-thirty or possibly five, a series of young men and older young men whose wavy hair and fixed expressions did not quite match their yet unchanged business suits, who would have looked, and would look after dinner, more fitting and comfortable in flowered shirts and slightly bulging blue jeans.

"It's a fag bar," he said softly to Madelaine. "Jones would-n't have been likely to come here."

Madelaine laughed. "It gets more mixed at night," she said not at all softly. "Anyway all men end up in gay bars when they get really goddamned drunk. Haven't you noticed?"

The bartender had noticed them and came over to the end of the bar where they were standing. He was heavy and Italian and did not look as if he belonged with the rest of the bar. "Hello, folks," he said. Madelaine and Ralston sat down on the barstools. "Let's both just have a glass of beer," Madelaine said. "I feel logy."

"We don't have tap beer, lady," the bartender said. "Only bottled. I'll get you both a Miller's."

"Only one," said Madelaine firmly. "And two glasses."

The bartender grunted and walked away to the other end of the bar. "You might have let me decide what I wanted," Ralston said. "You're not *my* wife."

Madelaine ignored him. The bartender had come back with the bottle of beer and two glasses. "Here you are, lady," he said. Ralston put fifty cents on the bar and the bartender rang all of it up on the register. He came back to face them. "We charge extra for two glasses," he said.

The nearest pair of wavy-haired young men tittered slightly. Ralston began to feel very uncomfortable. Madelaine, however, remained completely unconcerned. She poured half of the beer into Ralston's glass and half into her own. The bartender stood by watching. She took a sip of her beer and said to him, "We came in to ask you if a friend of ours happened to be in here just before closing time on Sunday night."

The bartender made an elaborate show of disgust. "Lady," he said, "what makes you even think I was here on Sunday night? I'm an afternoon and early evening bartender."

Madelaine looked disappointed. "Oh," she said. The bartender went away to serve another customer. He came back in a minute. "As a matter of fact I was tending bar here Sunday night," he said. "Frank was sick. Who's this friend you want to ask about?"

Madelaine was thoughtful. "You couldn't help noticing him if you saw him," she said. "He's a very tall and thin Negro. About six foot six. He probably was very drunk."

"And he looks a bit like Abraham Lincoln," Ralston added.

The bartender stared at Ralston and then he turned back to Madelaine. "Why do you think he was here?"

"We don't particularly," Madelaine said. "We're covering all the bars in Sausalito."

The bartender grunted again. "How many bars have you been to so far?"

"This is the first."

"And you're going to go to every bar in Sausalito hoping to find an evening bartender in the afternoon?"

Madelaine's face assumed a suspiciously humble expression. "I don't see what else we can do," she said sadly. "Do you have any suggestions?"

"Oh, he was here," the bartender said disgustedly. "You don't have to bother anybody else about it. He was here from one until closing time asleep in that booth over there. I'd have kicked him out if I hadn't been so busy."

"Did you notice if he made a phone call?"

"He was too fast asleep to make anything."

"Do you know what happened to him after the bar closed?" Madelaine asked.

"A customer managed to wake him up and drag him out before I called the police. I couldn't wake him myself."

"Do you know where we can get hold of the man that was with him?" Ralston asked, feeling that he should contribute something to the interrogation.

For the first time the bartender looked suspiciously at them. "Just what kind of deal is this?" he asked. "If you know the guy, why can't you ask him who he went home with?"

Madelaine put on her most mollifying smile. "It's a sort of a bet," she said. "Johnny — that's his name — couldn't remember where he'd been since eight o'clock Sunday evening until he woke up in his own bed Monday morning. We'd been talking about detective stories and my husband and I bet him five dollars that we could retrace his steps and tell him exactly where he'd been. He started in Palo Alto too."

"God!" the bartender said.

"So," Madelaine continued, "if we can get the name of the man who was with him maybe we can find out how he got back to Palo Alto."

"Like a scavenger hunt," the bartender said with some awe. "How many bars have you traced him to so far?"

"All over San Francisco," Madelaine said in the voice of a woman who would be engaging in a scavenger hunt. "And now here."

The bartender looked very carefully into both of their faces. "You look like you're really on the level," he said. "It was Oz Hamr. H-A-M-R. I don't know why he spells it that way. He runs a jewelry shop a block up the street. You didn't hear it from me. One of the customers told you."

"Thank you," Madelaine said. She gulped the rest of her beer and stood up. "Come on, Jim. Let's catch him before he closes up his shop." She smiled at the bartender. "Thank you for your help. We'll come back and tell you how we did." They left, Ralston sheepishly following Madelaine's aggressive lead.

When they got outside Ralston turned on her. "Of all the ridiculous performances," he said. "Myrna Loy in *The Thin Man*!"

"It worked, didn't it?" Madelaine said complacently.

"And that embarrassing business about the beer — and pretending that I was your husband."

Madelaine was very patient. "All of that was planned," she said. "Look, do you really think that all we would have had to do was to go into the bar and ask questions? Why should the bartender have told us anything? We might have been private detectives or Alcoholic Control Board people or something like that. We had to make him think we were harmless first. A nice screwy married couple playing games."

"And I suppose that business about the beer made us look like a typical married couple?"

"I thought that was a stroke of genius," Madelaine said brightly. "Could you imagine a couple of private detectives or two ABC officers ordering a single beer and two glasses? That clinched it with the bartender. We were harmless."

Ralston did not believe a word of it. "Then why did you start by ordering two draft beers?"

"Oh, I looked first to see that there wasn't any beer tap. It all went perfectly. Now if Sonia sends anyone over to check, the bartender will only remember a Negro from Palo Alto."

There was only one jewelry shop down the block and it was closed. The sign on the window said VOLUND'S in big ornamental gothic letters and they almost passed the shop as the wrong one until Madelaine noticed that "Oswald Hamr, Proprietor" was lettered at the bottom of the window in neat modern script. But it was the contents of the window that they stared at. There were exactly two objects in it — a large ornamental sword suspended from the top of the window point downward by a strand of white rope and, below the sword, a large goblet inlaid with what seemed to be ivory which was shaped and exactly proportioned to resemble a skull. The eyes, mouth, and other orifices were stopped with what, from their size, could only be imitation jewels. The effect was, in every sense, ghastly.

Ralston continued to be angry about what he considered Madelaine's still inexplicable behavior at the bar. "It would be something like this," he said. "It couldn't be a simple jewelry shop with rings in the window." It was almost, he thought while he was saying this, as if he blamed *her* for the skull.

Madelaine, however, was concerned neither with the skull or his anger. "His home address must be in the phone book," she said. "Or perhaps there's a card on the door."

There was a card on the door. It was also neatly, but more freely, lettered. "Oswald Hamr, Expensive Jewelry," it said. "Hours Irregular. Call at #12 Landing 7 If Shop Is Closed." "A houseboat," Madelaine said. "He lives on one of those houseboats that are anchored in the harbor. Let's go find him."

"What are we going to disguise ourselves as this time?" Ralston asked. "*Life* photographers?"

Madelaine turned her back on him and started walking quickly toward the waterfront. Ralston followed. When he was just a step behind her she said, "I wish I hadn't brought you along. You spoil things."

"For God's sake, Madelaine —"

"Even Arthur would have been better. He'd have monopolized everything but he wouldn't have resented our having a little fun."

"I thought you were serious about this," Ralston said, feeling that at least here he had trapped her. "If you admit that it's just a game —"

"A person can be serious and have fun, too." She slackened
her pace so that she was no longer a step ahead of him. "You
did all that talking in the bar about the sense of freedom
children have. Well, that's what they do." She waited a moment for Ralston to speak. He remained obstinately silent.
"Really Jim, you've gotten so stuffy since you've been in Boston. You think everything is dead serious or else a big fraud.
You can't see how they can be both at the same time."

"And you can?"

"I could never have raised a family if I couldn't."

Landing 7 was only a few blocks away. It, like the other
landings next to it, consisted of a wide pier against which on
both sides houseboats of almost every variety were anchored.
A few of these were old ships on whose decks cabins (house-
type cabins) had been constructed. These were the exceptions.
Most of the rest seemed to be actual houses that had merely
been transplanted, caulked, and made to float. They gave, as
Ralston and Madelaine walked down the pier, a very disassoci-
ated effect. They simply did not belong where they were. The
television antennas that rose from the roofs of nearly half of
them somehow completed their isolation. The front porch of
one of them anchored by the next pier — for the fronts of
them, or what on land would be the fronts of them, faced the
water instead of the piers on which they were anchored —
contained two canvas-backed chairs and a dog who was bark-
ing at the empty water. Ralston shuddered, half from the
sudden chillness of the early evening air and half from the
thought that the dog, where he was, was more of a prisoner
than if he had been locked in some small dark closet. He
pointed. "Look at that," he said to Madelaine.

Madelaine seemed to sense his thought. "I'm sure the dog
doesn't take it as seriously as you do, " she said. "Come on,
Number 12 must be just over here on the other side."

Ralston had so confidently expected the houseboat they
were looking for to be bizarre — to be, in the realm of houseboats, what Mr. Hamr's window was in the realm of jewelry
shop windows — that he was almost convinced that they were
on the wrong pier or that there were two houseboats num-
bered 12. It looked merely like a floating cabin from a medi-
um-sized motor court. Even its color, faded olive green with an

under-trace of brown, was in no way distinctive. They walked down the short catwalk to the door, Madelaine at least two feet ahead of Ralston.

A severely crew-cutted young man wearing blue jeans and a T-shirt opened the door. He rather glared at them. His appearance was pleasant but disconcerting. He looked more or less like a very young ex-marine or someone whose picture appears in the papers because he has, for no apparent reason, murdered an old lady. Madelaine was disconcerted, "Mr. Hamr —" she said.

"Sid," the young man yelled, turning back from the door. "It's for you." He disappeared leaving them standing at the threshold looking through the partly open door into a well furnished room.

Fully another minute passed before anyone else appeared. Finally, a small, thin, but powerfully built man with silver-gray hair whose age could have been anywhere between forty and sixty came slowly but hospitably up to greet them. He was wearing brown tweed slacks and a red shirt. "Good evening," he said in an accent which was almost, but not quite, standard British English. "Good evening. May I help you? You want to inquire about something in the shop perhaps?" He was looking as he spoke not to Madelaine but behind her at Ralston.

"Not exactly," Madelaine said, putting on the same bewildered smile that had worked so successfully with the bartender. "We're looking for information."

Mr. Hamr, who had started to move away from the doorway to let them in, moved imperceptibly back into the doorway. "You are from a newspaper?" he asked pleasantly.

Madelaine, sounding a bit breathless, plunged into approximately the same story that she had told the bartender. They were a married couple, from San Jose this time, and they had made a bet with their friend, named correctly this time as Jones might have volunteered his name to Mr. Hamr, that they could trace all of his movements on that drunken Sunday night. A customer in the bar had given them Mr. Hamr's name and now they wanted to find out —

Mr. Hamr, who had been listening to her in what seemed to Ralston a progressively icy silence, now interrupted her. "That is the least adroit story I have ever heard," he said. "If

you are police officers, please show your credentials and I'll
cooperate. If you are not, leave and leave immediately."

"I must not have explained it well," Madelaine began again
a little desperately. "We simply want to find out —"

Mr. Hamr turned to Ralston, who was still standing un-
comfortably behind Madelaine on the catwalk. "Will you tell
your wife or your business associate or whatever she is that
she is please not to bother me any further. As you haven't met
my challenge for credentials you are obviously not police
officers. If you are private detectives, you are shockingly unfit
for your jobs. Good night."

He started to push the door closed. Ralston, who would
have thought that he would have been more pleased than
annoyed at the way things had developed (after all, Madelaine
certainly deserved this for her spurious triumph with the
bartender and for remarks to him about his inability to play
games such as this) found himself saying quite loudly, "Wait,
listen to me!"

Mr Hamr paused. "I'll give you one minute for your new
story," he said.

Ralston, speaking quickly, and, it seemed to him, persua-
sively, blurted out a capsule version of what had really happened. "And so we're trying to find out where he was," he
concluded. "We want to prove that he couldn't have been the
person that beat up this woman."

Mr. Hamr opened the door wider but still did not seem
disposed to let them in. "That was a much more interesting
story," he said. "I'm surprised that you didn't tell it the first
time. Assuming that you are telling the truth, just who exactly
are the both of you and where do you fit in?" Madelaine started to answer but Mr. Hamr silenced her with a gesture of his
head. "Be quiet, my dear," he said. "Let your husband speak."

"I'm afraid I'm not her husband either," Ralston said.
"That's another one of Madelaine's exaggerations. She's the
wife of Arthur Slingbot, the poet. He's a very good friend of
Jones and would be here himself if he weren't rehearsing with
a jazz band. I'm Jim Ralston and I'm another poet."

Mr Hamr was almost friendly again. "I'm afraid I haven't
heard of you. I don't keep up much with contemporary poetry
these days. I have heard of Slingbot." He turned to Madelaine.

"My dear, do you have a driver's license or something made out in your name? I hate to seem suspicious, but you must admit that I have some grounds for it."

Madelaine started to open her purse and then suddenly stopped. "I'm afraid my driver's license is made out in my maiden name," she said.

There was an embarrassing pause. Mr. Hamr began to edge the door closed again, suspicion on his face. It occurred to Ralston for the first time, and it interested him more than the situation that they were presently in, that Madelaine might not be legally married to Slingbot. Why else should the driver's license be in her maiden name? "It doesn't matter," Madelaine said to their joint silence. "Jim has identification."

"But his identification would be useless, wouldn't it?" Mr. Hamr asked in a somewhat malicious voice. "Since I have never heard of a poet named James Ralston. Unless you carry press clippings with you?"

Ralston, recalled to the present situation by this malice, grew angry. "Surely you don't think that private detectives or policemen or whatever people you're afraid of would invent as complicated a story as this? We're not after the crown jewels of Ruritania. We simply want to find an alibi if there is one for our friend Mr. Jones."

"I'm not afraid of anything," Mr. Hamr said. "I simply don't want to be bothered. But if your story is the truth — I'll tell you what, I'll ask you a question. Why is my store called Volund's? If you're a poet you ought to know the answer."

Ralston thought. The name did sound familiar. The *Beowulf*, German mythology —? "The *Eddas*," he said suddenly. "He was in the *Eddas* somewhere."

"And what was he?"

Ralston thought again. This time no memory meshed. "I suppose I could guess that he was a craftsman of some sort but I don't really know."

"I suppose that's good enough," Mr. Hamr said and Ralston felt he was back at the committee of his qualifying examination for his Ph.D. "Disappointing but enough. Come on in and I'll get you a beer and tell you all you want to know." He showed them in and seated them both on a very small couch at one end of the room. "Skippy!" he called into the closed door of the room on his right and the crew-cutted young man appeared, still in T-shirt and blue jeans. Mr. Hamr reached into his wallet, took out a bill of some denomination, and gave it to him. "Go out somewhere and have a beer," he said.

Skippy took the bill without a word or a change of expression. He went out the front door, not even glancing at Ralston and Madelaine. Mr. Hamr moved towards the door of a room on the left which was evidently a kitchen. "I'll get the beers," he said.

"Won't he be cold without a coat?" Madelaine asked, but Mr. Hamr either ignored or did not hear the question.

When they were all settled with their beer (it was, and Ralston was somehow not surprised, imported German) Mr. Hamr cleared his throat. "I hope we're talking about the same person," he said. "I had the impression that he called himself Mr. Judge."

"Judge is his nickname," Madelaine said.

"Oh," Mr. Hamr looked at her with less distaste than he had previously shown but with no great enthusiasm. "That was one reason I was a bit suspicious. That and your fanciful story."

"Then you do know what happened to him after the bars closed last Sunday night?" Ralston asked very quickly as he saw that Madelaine was ready to say something.

"Up to a point," Mr. Hamr said. "I'm afraid it may not be much help to you." He sipped at his beer. "I got this friend of yours out of the bar just after closing time and took him to an all-night coffee shop down the street. He was very drunk. He had a cup of coffee and a sandwich. I tried to talk with him. He's some kind of artist, isn't he?"

"He does wire sculpture," Madelaine said.

"Wire sculpture?" Mr. Hamr expressed astonishment. "I would have thought that he was a non-objective painter." He paused and considered the matter further. "At any rate, he wasn't very coherent. Finally he decided that he had to go back to some party in San Francisco that he'd left earlier and he borrowed a quarter from me to make a phone call. He couldn't get anyone to drive over to pick him up and so he got it into his mind that he was going to take a bus. I kept telling him that there were no buses running until six in the morning but he wouldn't listen. I left him waiting at the bus stop."

"You just left him there?" Madelaine asked.

"I couldn't reason with him. I had already offered to let him stay overnight at my place. I don't quite see what else I could have done."

"What time was this?" Ralston asked.

"It must have been at least three." Mr. Hamr moved a bit in his chair. "That's all. I suppose your friend could have been in the city by four if someone had given him a ride that late at night. I told you that it wouldn't be much help."

Madelaine, Ralston could see, was measuring the amount of beer left in both of their glasses in order to estimate her chances for an immediate but polite withdrawal. Evidently the signs seemed favorable. "You've been very helpful," she said, pouring all that was left of the beer into her glass and drinking half of it. "It was very nice of you."

Ralston, whose cue had been so precisely, so finally given, had no intention of leaving quite yet. The beer was pleasant, the inevitable fight with Madelaine (which would end up, he supposed, with his kissing her) was unpleasant. "We're quite grateful to you," he said. "That window of your shop," he went on. "We looked for you there first. That window was really the strangest thing I've seen in a long time."

Mr. Hamr smiled. Madelaine pursed her lips. "You don't see the significance of the window?" Mr. Hamr asked.

"No." Ralston poured some but not all of the beer from the bottle into his glass slowly. "The sword and the skull are both beautiful but I doubt if you're going to sell either of them in Sausalito. I wondered what they mean." (And Ralston here, unconsciously as he saw it later, tried to push away from the atmosphere of the physical detective story that Madelaine — even unsuccessful Madelaine — had enveloped him with back to the metaphysical detective story that he and Rue and the Jungian Dr. Somebody had been enjoying passively at the bar. He actually expected, subconsciously as he saw it later, something important to happen from his question.)

"Paraphernalia," Mr. Hamr said. "Sheer paraphernalia. The story of Volund that you didn't know but recognized vaguely as coming from one of the *Eddas*. And my life. I'd better get you both another beer if you really want to hear the story."

"No more for me," Madelaine said. She looked at her watch. It was getting sleepy time, Ralston thought unkindly, for true detectives. He, in turn, slightly nodded to Mr. Hamr and felt that the gesture was enough not only to acquiesce in whatever was to be told him but also enough to act as an apology for Madelaine's rudeness.

Mr. Hamr was soon back with two beers which were duly opened and deposited in front of Ralston and himself. "Some wine, my dear?" Mr. Hamr said to Madelaine. She shook her head and he sat down and began his story.

"I have a nasty taste for parable in both my art and my life. I suppose you people, being poets or wives of poets and from San Francisco, can't imagine how someone who merely constructs things out of wood and metal can have to do with either art or parable —"

"Not at all," Madelaine said quickly. "I've seen some African masks and Kwakiutl wood carvings —"

"It was merely a rhetorical statement, my dear," Mr. Hamr interrupted in turn. "I am going to tell a story and don't give a damn if you people who have intruded into my house — though you are quite welcome here at the moment — understand it or not. Imagine, and be damned to your Kwakiutl igloos or whatever they are, that a man who hammers metal or carves wood is an artist." He took a small cigar out of the breast pocket of his shirt and lit it. He inhaled deeply and blew the smoke out of his mouth. "Volund," he said slowly, "was a man who made things out of metal. He lived a long time ago. He kept his forge and lived in the middle of a large forest. This would have been safe enough today and I suppose that only a few Boy Scouts and bird-watchers would have stumbled across him and maybe bought a knife or a belt buckle, but in those days the forests were well traveled. There were only a few roads in and out and people were using them all the time. And people would often stumble across Volund as they used the road that was near to his forge. He would sell them something if they carried gold or some other precious metal or exchange them something if they were commercial travellers or give them something if they were monks or beggars. All in all it was a good life.

"One day the king and queen of some unimportant place were travelling through the forest. The queen, like all other people that passed along the road, saw the smoke from his forge and the small side-road that led to it, and, like most of them, was curious and wanted to investigate. She persuaded the king and the guards that were with them to go along with her and see what was happening.

"They found him there at his forge, blowing at the fire with his bellows, cursing a bit at the wood that did not burn properly. Suspended from the top of the workshop was a sword, a sword that he had just finished. It seemed to the queen, and to the king when she mentioned it to him, the most beautiful sword that she had ever seen in the world." Mr. Hamr paused and looked at Ralston. "You look like you have a question," he said. "Interrupt me any time. After all, it isn't my allegory."

"I was wondering why he put his forge so close to the path," Ralston said. "If he didn't want people to notice the smoke."

"He explained that," Madelaine said. (She *liked* stories.) "He had to do some business so he could buy more metals. He wasn't afraid of his customers."

"That's enough of an answer for the moment," Mr. Hamr said. "Though I agree it needs more explaining. But, after all, the fact of the beautiful sword — and it was beautiful, I'll swear to that — was more important than all of Volund's motives.

"Volund was quite willing to sell them the sword. He could use the gold with which they would pay for it and buy some other metals with it too — but in the middle of the bargaining the queen began to get another idea. 'We don't have a smith of our own,' she said to the king. 'This man has made the most beautiful sword in the world and he is likely to make others. Why don't we take him with us and let him be our personal craftsman?' She turned to Volund. 'We will let you have a much better workshop than this one and you will dine at the same table with the rest of our courtiers.'

"'I'm quite happy here,' Volund said, becoming frightened because he knew that what kings and queens decided on

usually happened. 'Take the sword with you as my gift and I
promise never to make another of the same design. I give the
sword to you out of my appreciation of the kindness of your
offer. And if there are any other trinkets you care to take
before you leave. This jeweled dagger, for instance.'

"'You are coming with us!' the queen said flatly. She mo-
tioned the nearest of the bodyguards forward. At that moment
Volund tried to run but they pinned him down. They bound
him and carried him with them the fifty miles to the palace.

"The queen had been sincere about the offer of the better
forge and the table with the rest of the courtiers, but the king
was more practical. 'This fellow would just try to run away
again and even if he didn't he would hardly be good company
in the palace.' They decided to hamstring his legs and build a
workshop for him on a little island out in the middle of the
bay. There he could work and not run away and they could
send a boat once a week to bring him provisions and to take
away whatever new swords or daggers or drinking cups he had
made. 'It was not,' the king said, 'as if they were punishing
him. He would have as much freedom as he had had in the
forest and would have better food.'"

"He should have never tried to escape so soon," Ralston
said. "He should have waited until they thought he liked it in
the palace and then tried to escape."

"The story does not make Volund a very practical man,"
Mr. Hamr said. "If he had been capable of thinking that far
ahead, perhaps he would never have wanted to escape from
the king and queen in the first place. At any rate, they ham-
strung him and put him on the island. And he worked at the
new forge. Although it was difficult to hobble around at first,
he learned how to manage it and was soon making as many
swords and daggers and drinking cups as he had made before.
He passed several years this way, meeting the boat that was
sent once a week, unloading the provisions and supplies, and
loading it up in turn with finished works of metal and wood.
But all this time he had been working on a pair of wings —
artificial wings that he could attach to his powerful shoulders
so that he could fly away and escape from the island."

"What were they made of?" Madelaine asked, pulling Ralston out of that state of half-sleep that the rhythmic rocking of the boat and story itself had begun to induce.

"I don't know," Mr. Hamr said, showing no sign that he felt interrupted. "I have often wondered. But he did finish the wings and on several tests they worked well enough. He had tried them for short distances on the island and he was resting in the late afternoon and he decided to use them to attempt to escape to the mainland on the very next morning.

"It was then that he saw someone swimming through the light surf towards the island. The figure became more distinct. It was a boy of about fifteen. He was swimming easily. He reached the beach in about five minutes. Volund limped over to the edge of the sand where the boy was shaking water out of his long hair. 'Where have you come from?' Volund asked. 'Are you shipwrecked?'

"'I am your apprentice,' the boy said. 'I am the king's only son. I have seen your daggers and your swords and your drinking cups at the palace and I want to learn how to make wood and metal beautiful in the way you do. I ran away from the palace and swam here to find you. I want to stay here and learn to work metal like you do.'

"'The king doesn't know you've come here?' Volund asked.

"'No one knows that I've come here,' the boy said. 'No one will have to know. I can hide when the supply boat comes. My father will never suspect that I'm with you.'

"Volund stared back at him. He looked very much like his father. 'Don't send me back,' the boy pleaded. 'I can set your fires at first and work the bellows. I want to learn how to be a swordsmith.'

"The boy was shivering and naked while he said this. Volund limped off and brought him a rag to wipe himself with and a clout and a shirt to wear. Then he led him into the workshop. 'Are you really the king's son?' he asked wonderingly. The boy looked him full in the face. 'I was once the king's son. I am now your apprentice,' he answered.

"Volund showed him around the workshop, showed him the uncast metals, the jewels, the breastplate which now finished was just in the process of cooling. The wings were resting against one of the benches but, not being on Volund's shoulders, their purpose was not obvious and the boy did not bother to question him about them or Volund to explain them.

"Finally Volund pointed to a large chest. 'This chest,' he said, 'contains the greatest of all my treasures. Look into it.' The boy opened the heavy metal chest and bent down to look into it. At that moment Volund took up one of his light swords and sliced the boy's head off.'"

Mr. Hamr took a large sip of beer and looked at both of them. Just, in a way, like Mr. Hashiwara, Ralston thought. No one here wants you to guess when a story is really over. He was silent and Madelaine was silent and Mr. Hamr began to speak again:

"He buried the body of the king's son deep in the sand and burned the skull in his furnace until nothing but bone was left. Then he powdered the bone and mixed it with molten silver and molded the silver until it was the exact shape of the boy's skull. He plugged up all the openings of the skull, except for a rim at the top, with the finest jewels the king had given him for decoration. It was a drinking cup. I think it looked a little bit like the drinking cup I display in my window." Mr. Hamr paused again. "I'm sorry that I can't tell you what the rest of the story was," he said. "The text of the *Edda* that it's in gets corrupt at this point. Perhaps you would like to guess at the ending." He settled back into his chair and sipped again at his beer.

"I think that Volund must have put the drinking cup into the boat the next morning with a message to the king telling him exactly what it was made of," Madelaine said. "And then put on his wings and flown back to the forest which he came from. Otherwise there wouldn't be much point to the story."

Mr. Hamr grinned and looked at Ralston, who felt that he was being examined again. "I'm not sure," he said. "I think he'd have to use the wings and the drinking cup in the same operation. Perhaps he put on the wings and flew across the bay and above the palace and dropped the drinking cup at the feet of the king and queen, shouting at them from the sky exactly what he had done with their son. And perhaps," for the story did sound melodramatic to Ralston as he told it, "he didn't have enough strength left in his shoulders to keep the wings moving much longer and he had to crash or fly back to the island."

"A just ending," Mr. Hamr said, smiling again. "That's the nice thing about incomplete myths. One can impart justice to them. My own idea is that Volund carefully burned the wings and put the drinking cup on the boat the next day without any explanation and that no one ever found out what happened to the king's son." He drained the last of his second bottle of beer and became brisk. "I'm sorry I won't be able to give you any more of my time. I want to write some letters before Skippy gets back." They started to rise — Ralston immediately and Madelaine more slowly. "Not this very second," Mr. Hamr said. "I do hate to seem a poor host, but if I hadn't said something rude like that I would have started to tell you another story. I usually only have customers to talk to. Do you have any more questions about your friend?" The question was directed at Madelaine and she shook her head. "About the story then? I'll let you each have one question about the story."

Since the time the story was over Ralston had found himself not paying much attention. He was unaccountably worrying and feeling guilty about the manuscript of Rue's poetry in his room that he had not read. There *had* been a question he wanted to ask. "Were the swords and the other things," he asked Mr. Hamr, "that Volund produced on the island as beautiful as those that he produced in the forest?"

"The story doesn't say," said Mr. Hamr. "Don't ask me. I didn't see either of them. Now," turning to Madelaine, "Your question."

"Is your name really Oswald Hamr?"

"No." Mr. Hamr did not seem disconcerted by the question though Ralston certainly was. "It's Sidney Hammer. HAMMER. I was born in Cheapside, London. My father was a goldsmith and so was his father." He stood up, forcing them to rise with him. "I am glad that I have been able to help you somewhat. Good night."

They escaped with muttered and hurried thanks. Madelaine was unaccountably silent in the car and refused Ralston's offer of dinner with the observation that Arthur would have something waiting for her. She obviously wanted merely to drive him across the bridge and to his hotel and she did just that. She seemed, it seemed to Ralston, a little bewildered and a little hurt.

Ralston had his own dinner by himself. Bad spaghetti in a Market Street restaurant. He had consumed the last half of the bottle of brandy and the last half of *The Temptation of St. Anthony* before he went to sleep. That night he had a long complicated dream of which he could remember only that it involved Rue disappearing down a rabbit hole and (in the rabbit hole?) Madelaine and Ralston coming upon Mr. Hamr in a wizard's suit sitting at a card table. He had a greasy deck of cards before him, and, though he did not touch the cards during the dream, he offered to tell both of their fortunes for them. Ralston asked him, with some undefinable emotion of regret, if they would both find what they were looking for. Mr. Hamr, if it was still Mr. Hamr below the wizard's cap, replied in a surprisingly feminine voice, "The question is meaningless. Neither of you is looking for anything."

VII

Ralston was lost. He was sitting on a bench in a small park near the top of a hill. Nothing was visible to him but a kind of cliff (or was it merely an incline?) which was covered on one side with just enough trees and bushes to block his vision of what, if anything, was at the bottom of it. From the other three sides large apartment houses rose and only a thin vertical line of sky, and what must be a part of the bay, could be seen between them.

He was exhausted. This was the third hill, if he had not somehow repeated hills, that he had rested at the top of, wondering if, this time, he would find North Beach at its bottom. The sky above him was brilliant and very light blue and the few clouds in it, which drifted along on their absurd, delicate shapes, managed to create the impression that they too were lost and were ambling along the top of the sky looking for their own cloudy equivalent of North Beach.

He had woken up in the morning feeling very much like he had for those terrible few minutes in The Birdcage on the previous afternoon. The feeling was milder — therefore, since it was less likely to be mere depression, more convincing. When he reached into the drawer for a clean shirt and discovered that he had no more clean shirts and that he had not yet sent his dirty shirts to the laundry, he suddenly reached a decision. He would not send his shirts to the laundry. He did not want to have to stay in San Francisco the length of time it would take to get his shirts back from the laundry. He would leave San Francisco (not perhaps to go back to Boston immediately or even at all that summer, and Anne had already left for Paris and he could not reasonably, even from the standpoint of Anne's reason, now follow her, but he could leave San Francisco today, that very afternoon in fact, for Los Angeles where he still had relatives, or for Seattle where he had several good friends, or — but this would be easy to decide later in the morning), he would leave San Francisco and Madelaine, and the silly mystery about Judge, and the shirts, and the unread manuscript of Rue's poetry — he would, and discovered that there was joy in his heart, leave San Francisco immediately.

At that moment the telephone in his room rang. He would not answer it. It was bound to be Madelaine, or Henry, or someone else who would want him to do something or be something which he did not want to do or want to be. He would not let any of them know that he was leaving. He would write them. He began packing his soiled shirts keeping the cleanest one of them to wear into the smallest of his suitcases. He almost packed the envelope containing Rue's poetry in with them until he realized what it was. He would have to give that back. Unread, it was enough of an insult. He would have to take it back to Rue, or rather to Sonia's apartment where if he were lucky Rue would not be home, this very morning. He could even leave it outside the door —

He got up from the bench. How far he had walked he did not know. He had plenty of time, a whole summerful of time, and it did not matter if he left San Francisco at six o'clock or at midnight. For the first time since he had come to San Francisco he felt that he was on vacation, was being given a change from a very pleasant life that he could always go back to — And then, also for the first time since he had come to San Francisco, he felt like writing a poem. He sat back down on the bench, took out a small notebook which he always kept in his coat pocket, and began to write.

Two hours and several miles later he was sitting on another bench in another park. A rather small flat park at the base of North Beach. The poem had been twelve lines long when he left the park where he started it, seven lines long when he left a coffee shop halfway down the hill, and now, as he closed his notebook in this second and final park, the original twelve lines — reshaped and purified by the coffee shop surgery, were back again. There was a word here and there that was perhaps wrong — he would have to stare at each of them for days before he was certain — but the poem was not wrong and it was his. He opened the notebook and glanced at it again with satisfaction. It was one of *his* poems. A little alien perhaps, just as the face he looked at in the bureau mirror in his hotel room in San Francisco was not quite the same face that he had looked at in the bathroom mirror in Boston, a little changed, but *his*. All of this crap, all of this searching and talk of Blake and football games, all of this having a fish slammed at you was just the outer edges of the poem that you would really write. I am myself, Ralston thought with surprise, and my poems are my poems.

He got up from the bench and started to walk slowly in the direction — he recognized directions again — of Sonia's apartment. He could have almost changed his mind about leaving San Francisco, he thought to himself, if he did not recognize that the energy behind this poem, the mirror itself on which the poem was reflected, was the product of his leaving it. The Social Muse, the labyrinth of puzzles and pleasures in which all the artists he had met here were so happily turning, *bugged* him. He was himself and his poems were his poems and they had no connection and would not be improved by the kind of games other people were playing. The fourth quarter, if the whole image were not a mare's nest hatched by his *non*-poetic personality, could exist as well in the changing of one important word as it could in the summoning of angels. Beauty, after all, was beauty.

And Los Angeles. Or Mexico, he thought suddenly, the length of his stride increasing, where he could live cheaply for a while and be himself and write like himself and let the pace of his own development (his poetry's development) go its own way unaffected by anybody he was trying to keep up with. And let the Rues and the Slingbots and the Sonias and the Madelaines go to hell or to heaven in their own way. And he, to neither or to both, in his.

As he ascended the hill on which Sonia lived, walking even faster, he began not to care whether Rue was home, began rather to wish that he would be. He could hand him the sheaf of unread poems and tell him that he did not want to talk about them now, that he would write him a letter. (And, as a matter of fact, if he had read them, whether they were dreadful or good, could he have *talked* about them? Would he not have to have written Rue a letter?) And then from Los Angeles or Mexico he would write the letter explaining the circumstances. Explaining, in what could be a very beautiful letter, exactly why he could not have allowed himself to read the poems. Explaining (but not justifying) the temporary pseudo-

Jim Ralston that San Francisco had created for a few days.
And from that aesthetic distance (Los Angeles or Mexico or
even Boston) Rue might reply and they might exchange letters
and he, or the both of them, might learn enough about angels
to manufacture them in their own basements.

When he knocked on Sonia's door (which he found easily
this time) Sonia herself answered. All the bandages were off
except for a small cast on her right wrist. Her face, however,
was still puffy and discolored. "You have come back," she said.
"You have brought an offer from your friend who calls himself
a Judge?"

"No," Ralston said. In the moment of his triumph he had,
as a matter of fact, forgotten all about this silly business. "I
was wondering if I could leave some —" The sentence was to
have been completed "of the poems Rue gave me with you,"
but, although the rest of the words remained in his mind like
a subtitle in a foreign movie, his voice stopped completely as
he suddenly realized that the sheaf of Rue's poems he had
started out with was not in his hands, that he must have left
it where — in one of the anonymous parks, in the coffee shop
or had he really not started with it at all but of course he had
because he remembered having worried about the sweat of his
hands staining the outside of it as he was walking up the first
hill but, no, not later, he could not remember it later, he must
have had it when he was writing the poem but —

"Well," Sonia said. "Has the beast got your tongue?"

Ralston pulled himself together. He had to retrace his
altogether irretraceable steps immediately. He had to get out
of here and look for the manuscript. "Actually," he said, with
more calmness than he felt, "I was looking for Rue."

Sonia looked at him coldly. "He is here," she said. "He is
asleep on the bed but I will wake him up." She moved away
from the door before Ralston could stop her. "Baby," she yelled,
"you have a visitor. Wake up." Ralston could not see the bed
but she must have been shaking him. "Wake up, baby. You
have been sleeping on the bed for three hours now with your
shoes dirty." There was a grunt and then silence. Ralston
spoke from the doorway, "I'll come back," he started to say but
his words were covered by a splash of water and a great
cursing. " — bitch — " "And I'll fill another teapot full of water

and pour that down your pants too. Wake up. You have a guest."

Rue came to the door wearing a pair of very wet blue jeans and nothing else. His hair fell down onto his forehead and his face from at least seventeen directions. He was rubbing his eyes. Ralston noticed, even while he was planning escape, that Rue's body was much more tan and much more angular than he would have imagined. "It's you," Rue said, amiably but still half asleep. "Come in."

"I didn't mean to have her wake you," Ralston said. "I was just dropping by —"

"He said that he was dropping by to leave something and then he stopped," Sonia interrupted. "You are perhaps bringing Baby something you don't want me to know about? Baby and I have no secrets together, little man."

"Shut up and make some tea, Sonia," Rue said. He walked over to the dresser, took a pair of clean blue jeans from the top drawer, and casually took off the wet pair he had on.

Sonia paused from the teamaking that she had obediently started. "Isn't his body beautiful?" she asked Ralston, in exactly the tone she might have used to ask him to admire a painting. "Most Americans have fat muscles and look like they could never move them. My Baby looks like a prehistoric sparrow which is just about to fly."

Rue glared at her and put on the new pair of jeans more quickly than he had started to. He turned so that he fully faced Ralston who was now standing inside the doorway. "That's better," he said. "Sit down. Tea will be ready in a minute."

The whole scene registered on Ralston only very spottily. He had a horror of things lost, a certainty, whether they were a pencil or a sheaf of poems, that they could never be found, were, in fact, cunningly hidden by the very process of being lost. Anne was always the person to find things around the house (with many uncomfortable Freudian remarks about how they happened to be lost in the first place) and, even if he could do without Anne, he had never lost anything over so wide an area as he had lost these poems. And he had to return them before he could leave San Francisco without confessing he had lost them. That was certain. It would be impossible to say "I did not read your poems and I lost them." Besides, so sloppy was the boy's life (Rue at this point had thrown the wet pair of jeans on the floor and was putting on the new pair) that some of the poems were probably his only copies. He would have to find, though he despaired of the effort, exactly where he had left them. The most likely place would be the park where he had begun to write the poem, but —

So he sat down in the only chair in the room when Rue told him to sit down, too abstracted with the problem he had presented himself with (for Anne, and the people behind her, were undoubtedly right about the reason for people losing things) to even feel uncomfortable. "I wasn't really bringing anything," he said. "Sonia misunderstood me. I just dropped by. It's a nice day for walking."

Sonia turned angrily from her teamaking. "I cannot walk because of the injuries caused me by your friend the Judge," she said firmly. "And Baby is not going to leave me alone here to go walking."

"I didn't mean to go walking," Ralston said, looking a little nervously at Rue. "I meant that's why I was walking." Not only did he not know how, in what way, he was going to look for the lost manuscript, but he did not know how he was going to get out of this room in order to start looking for it. "I'm sorry you had to be woken up. I just wanted to drop by for a couple of minutes."

"The tea is ready," Sonia said. She handed a cup without a saucer to Ralston and a cup with a saucer to Rue. Her own tea she poured into a small soup bowl. "Now give your message from the Judge and his band of Storm Troopers, little man. I know you came here to threaten me."

Ralston considered for a moment whether a fight with Sonia and a hurt retreat would be the easiest method of exit. It would not. Rue would be sure to want to leave with him to apologize for Sonia and to ask whether he had read the poems. That would be more awkward than it was now. "No," he said. "That whole business is between you and Jones. It's not my concern."

Rue, who was half lying, half sitting on the bed, scratched his flat, hairless stomach. "The whole thing's a drag anyway," he said. "Sonia would get bored and forget all about it if people didn't seem so interested."

"I will not forget," Sonia said, sipping her tea savagely. "Bulgarians never forget. We do not forgive anything that happens to us." She stared hard at Ralston. "Remember that!"

If there was only someone he could borrow a car from, Ralston thought. With a car and with all the afternoon he might be able to find all the parks he had walked into — and the coffee shop. It was more likely to be the coffee shop. But Madelaine would ask questions and want to come along and he would have to tell her and she would, inevitably, find out that he planned to leave town and, also inevitably, at least spoil his leaving. And Henry had no car and would be curious anyway over what had happened to him and why he lost the poems. As a matter of fact he could not imagine anyone he had seen since he got here that it would be comfortable to look for the poems with. Except Mr. Hashiwara. Mr. Hashiwara, he thought wryly, would understand everything. Or Mr. Simpson. What he needed was a map of the city with the parks marked on it.

"— to turn on —," Rue was saying.

"What?"

"He looks like he has already been turned on," Sonia said. "Or maybe he's been smoking opium. Sadists always smoke opium."

"I was asking you if you'd like to turn on," Rue said patiently. "I have some real good shit."

— Or a taxi. He could take a taxi even if it might cost five or ten dollars. And he could tell the taxi driver that he had lost an important business document and get his kind of anonymous help. If he could only — He nodded his head to Rue who was saying something avant-garde and incomprehensible. Then, when he and the taxi driver had found the manuscript, he could leave the city with his own poem in his breast pocket.

Rue had taken something from behind the alarm clock. It looked, fuzzily to Ralston as he still was not paying attention, like a badly made hand-rolled cigarette. Both ends of it were twisted. Rue untwisted one end of it slightly and began to light it.

Suddenly, like a man noticing that the tide has come in all around him while he has been sleeping on a rock, Ralston realized what they had been talking about. They were going to smoke, had been inviting him to smoke, a marijuana cigarette. And, like the same man looks behind him from the rock and sees that the ocean has also covered his remaining retreat with water, he realized that the invitation was the question he had just nodded at.

If there was anything in the world he did not need now, here at two in the afternoon (it must be at least that) on the day he was leaving town and had lost and was yet, if it was possible, to find Rue's poetry, it was to smoke marijuana with Rue and Sonia. And a simple no, simple then because if he had been listening, even though he did not think he had heard exactly the phrase "turning on" before, he would have known, would certainly have known what Rue meant. And refused gracefully. But now, Rue was handing the joint to him and he knew that these things had to be smoked quickly before they burned away, but now — Rue's big fingers were transferring the thing to his smaller ones. He stared at it indecisively for a quarter of a second. Time, as it was supposed to afterwards and not before, stood still for the quarter of a second. Then, as unexpectedly as anything he had ever done, he put the half-full cup of tea he was still carrying in his left hand on the floor, slowly, for quarter seconds did not count now, plunged the marijuana cigarette into it with his right hand, and walked, neither slowly nor quickly, out of the astonished room.

When he came to himself in the corridor, for, it occurred to him, his mind had so exactly anticipated the symptoms of *turning on* that he had *turned on*, he heard Sonia's voice yelling and Rue's voice answering. They might, Rue might, still come after him. He ran down the stairs.

When he got outside (the few clouds in the sky had disappeared leaving a sky and a skyline of absolute clarity) he was amazed at his own behavior. Marijuana did not shock him. While he had never smoked it himself, he had watched people smoke it twice at parties in New York and once Anne and he had agreed, if they ever found anybody who had some, to try it together and discover, both for her benefit and for his, exactly what its effects were.

Ralston's panic (Anne would call it panic but he was damned if he'd call it that) abated at the thought of Anne. In the first place, she would say if she were walking beside him now, what panics you is the loss of the poems. Now are you sure that finding them is all that important? And was it? These couldn't be the only copies — not if they were at all important to Rue or, for that matter, to anybody. And if worse came to worst and they were the only copies, he would at least have the drafts of the poems he had revised them from and could reconstruct them easily. Unless he had just sat down at the typewriter and written the poems. In which case they were valueless anyway. And Rue would merely think that he had become panicked by the marijuana or by him and in either case be flattered and not offended. And he would be out of town and would never have to explain. The whole panic (Anne's word, not his) was ridiculous. He would forget about the whole thing and go about making his plane reservations.

But Jim, Anne's voice once summoned up could not be stilled, now you're overreacting the other way. First you want to rush around the town in a taxi looking for the poems like they're the crown jewels and now you want to ignore them completely. Be sensible. At least look in that last park and the coffee shop you went to. That's where they probably are anyway. You're always so — But Ralston started walking more quickly and managed almost to unsummon her voice.

It was just before he reached the park that he noticed the headline of the newspaper. Actually it was not so simple a process as noticing a headline and reading it. Two blocks earlier, still pursued by faint echoes of Anne's voice and the panic that had preceded her voice, the word "BEATNIK" had jumped out at him from a newspaper headline. And this had given him a new, if allied, train of thought. Among the many reasons Slingbot had listed that Washington Jones would be tried and condemned in an atmosphere of prejudice was what he called "the *Post*'s phony beatnik scare." Ralston had dismissed Slingbot's whole explanation of the cryptic phrase as sheer paranoia, but there the word was. The *Post*, an afternoon newspaper in a town where most people only read morning newspapers, had found a new crusade and new circulation in attacking the manners and the morals of the inhabitants of

North Beach's Bohemia. The word (Slingbot had here launched on a confusing dissertation on the symbolic impact of the Russian Sputnik on the American middle class) was derived from the phrase "beat generation" — Ralston had seen that in both Slingbot's and Rexroth's articles on San Francisco poetry and it was used by the *Post* (and all the other San Francisco papers with varying degrees of enthusiasm) to describe the participants in the incredible artistic (the *Chronicle* used the word "existentialist") orgies that went on in North Beach. Ralston who had never seen anyone in North Beach do anything more orgiastic than drink other people's beer with the exception of today — and if marijuana counted, a full half of the Puerto Rican and Negro population of New York were also beatniks — was curious what the *Post* could possibly say, how the small, overcomplicated adventures of the people he had seen could be really headlined. Before he started looking for the poetry manuscript, at the next newsrack he passed as a matter of fact, he would buy a *Post* and read the news story. It would be another way of saying goodbye.

It was not until he had reached the park in which he had finished his poem that he could find another newsrack that was not empty. "BEATNIK POET DIES ON FIRE ESCAPE," the headline read. For a second he thought of Rue and then realized that he had just seen Rue. Nevertheless, he sat down on the park bench and opened the news story like a telegram:

The broken body of Washington Jones, 26, self-styled member of the beat generation, was discovered early this morning on the second story fire-escape of the North Beach hotel in which he lived. Police reported that the cause of death was a broken neck probably caused by a fall from the fire-escape next to Jones' room three stories above. They declined to speculate whether the fall was accidental, self-inflicted, or the result of foul play. Police Captain Vernon Watkins, in charge of the investigation, allowed himself to be quoted as saying, "We are leaving no stone unturned. These so-called beatniks cause us more trouble than any other element in the city. If anyone was with Jones when he fell, we want to find out who it was."

The story, a stop-press item, ended there. Ralston's first reaction was to wonder why on earth they said that Washington Jones was a poet and his second to wonder if the messy investigation that would undoubtedly ensue would prevent him from leaving town. Should he call Slingbot? Should he pretend not to have read the paper? The police, after all, would not visit — Then it suddenly occurred to him whom the police would visit. Almost immediately. Perhaps even now had visited. Sonia's name was on the police department records with the complaint against Washington Jones. They would be coming to her apartment and would find her there with Rue smoking, or at least in possession of marijuana cigarettes. He had to warn them quickly. He looked around for a taxi.

There was no taxi and as he started walking quickly up Columbus Avenue in the general direction of their house, he wondered whether he should really take a taxi if one appeared. Suppose the police were already there. What excuse could he make for having taken a taxi? For that matter (and this, he saw after a moment's reflection, was the only crucial question anyway) what excuse could he give the policeman for visiting them?

This makes up for my losing his poetry, Ralston said to himself half in jest, as a taxi appeared and he took it. Nevertheless he had the taxi stop at the corner and not in front of the house and, before he entered the building, he looked carefully around, making sure that none of the parked cars belonged to the police.

No one answered when he knocked on the door. He knocked again and again wondering if Sonia and Rue were in bed together or not answering the door because they were still smoking the marijuana or whether the police had already been here and taken them away. "It's me, Jim Ralston," he yelled through the door. "Wake up." (He thought that was a tactful way of putting it no matter what they were doing.) "Wake up. It's an emergency."

There was a distant sound of giggling from inside the room, an ambiguous noise or two, and then the door opened and Rue appeared on the threshold. He was wearing an old white shirt now within his pair of jeans. "So you're back," he said. Then he giggled.

Sonia giggled in accompaniment. "Welcome back, Mr. Poor
of Spirit and Meek of Heart," she said. "We was just having a
fight about you."

Ralston, who felt sure that they were about to tell him just
what they had been saying, broke in quickly. "Judge is dead,"
he told them, speaking almost over Rue's shoulder so Sonia
could be included. "He fell off a fire-escape last night and
broke his neck."

Rue laughed this time, a hearty laugh instead of a giggle.
Three buttons of his shirt were unbuttoned. "You're just trying
to bug me," he said. "Come in and sit down."

Ralston, who at the moment would have given anything to
have had the paper with him (he had thrown it in the trash
can just before he took the taxi on the thought that it would
not be nice to have it with him if he ran into the police) tried
again. "I'm not joking," he said. "You've got to sober up and
listen. It's in this afternoon's *Post*. The police are going to
investigate everybody. They don't know how he died."

"I thought you said he broke his neck," Sonia said from the
inside of the room. She crooned the words to herself afterwards in a mock operatic style. "I thought you said he broke
his neck. I thought you said he broke his neck. I thought you
said he broke his neck."

"Shut up," Ralston yelled, looking to the stairway from
which at any minute he expected to see policemen emerging.
"Shut up!" He took hold of Rue's shoulders and shook him,
vaguely glad at the moment that Rue had put on a shirt. "I'm
not joking. Judge is dead. The police may be coming at any
moment to ask Sonia questions. You'd better get rid of that
stuff and get out of here until you're sober enough to face
them."

"You say *down*, not *sober*, for that," Rue said, but Ralston
could see that he was beginning to believe him.

Ralston shook him again. "The police will be coming.
You've got to straighten up and get out of here."

Panic replaced incredulous amusement on Rue's face.
"You're not joking, are you?" He put his hand on Ralston's
shoulder as if to steady himself. "I think I hear someone on
the stairs now." He turned quickly, his hand almost hitting

Ralston across the face as he spun. "Sonia, hide that stuff away quickly. Throw it out the window or something."

"I have already put it in the teapot," Sonia said calmly. "The tobacco and the butts that you call roaches. It will be very hard to dry but the police will never find it."

Ralston, standing in the doorway, wished for that moment that he could see Sonia's face or remember it. He was suddenly conscious of her as a woman. Like Anne in a way — though Anne would have had neither the marijuana or the teapot. But in spite of her hideousness (but he could not remember what Sonia's body would look like either) she really was, must be, like Anne. He felt engulfed in a wave of tenderness, as he often was, he noticed as he felt it, when he had been confronted with too many conflicting emotions in the space of too few hours. He almost could not hear what Rue was saying. "You silly bitch, you silly bitch," Rue was saying. "Don't you know that that's exactly where they'll look?" And Sonia just stood there smiling, puffed face and bandages and all — looking in all of her smallness like some huge Slavic goddess.

"Let's get Rue out of here and get him some coffee," Ralston said finally. "He's not in any shape to talk to policemen if they do come."

Sonia became Sonia again. "I will take care of him," she said. "Thank you for your interest." Rue was now sitting on the bed crying. Ralston left.

AFTERWORD

Jack Spicer had great hopes for the detective novel he began in San Francisco in the spring of 1958, which we have titled *The Tower of Babel* after its hero's memorable dream in chapter three. In this book Spicer planned to take advantage of public interest in the "Beat Generation" by satirizing that interest, turning it upside down, holding a mirror to the public's own face. He would make money, too, or so he believed. He had always loved detective novels and now, at age thirty-three, this genre formed the bulk of his reading.

Like many intellectuals, Spicer found his enjoyment of mystery and detective stories something of a guilty pleasure, but he defended them passionately as he did baseball. When other poets scoffed, Spicer would proffer Yeats as an example of a great poet who read mysteries too. (He was never contradicted, though his evidence was dubious.) His favorites were the "hard-boiled" novels of Dashiell Hammett and Raymond Chandler (both still writing in 1958, although Hammett had long since ceased to publish), but his tastes were omnivorous. Readers of *The Tower of Babel* will notice a certain resemblance to Fredric Brown's *Alice*-inspired *Night of the Jabberwock* (1952), and surely the independence and spirit of Madelaine Cross are drawn from Dorothy Sayers' Harriet Vane, and to a lesser extent from Georgia Strangeways, the heroine invented by "Nicholas Blake" (C. Day Lewis) in a series of English thrillers. Fellow Berkeley students have indicated that Spicer met "½ of Ellery Queen" at a literary soiree in the late forties. Another fan of detective stories was W. H. Auden, whom Spicer had met in October of 1954 during the senior poet's visit to San Francisco to inaugurate the Poetry Center there. Perhaps Spicer has Ralston give his name — in chapter one — as "W. H. Auden" as a tip of the hat to Auden's famous defence of the detective story, "The Guilty Vicarage," in which Auden had argued the fictional sleuth is really the priest of the twentieth century, restoring order out of chaos.

Spicer began his novel with confidence, but the process of fictionalizing his experience among the Beats quickly grew problematic. By the fall of 1958 he had abandoned the novel to his typist, Robert Duncan, and his editor, Donald Allen, who was entrusted with finding an agent. When a publisher bought the book, he declared, he would finish it to everyone's satisfaction.

This was not to happen, and it's easy to see why, thirty-five years later. *The Tower of Babel* is a parable of spiritual exhaustion and a "Textbook of Poetry," as well as a genre novel.* Coming so late in the story, a headline rather than an event, the death of Washington Jones is a bewildering culmination of a picaresque narrative line. Murder? Suicide? Accident? It's as though Spicer were thumbing his nose at the conventions of the Detective Club, those he was so quick to defend against the jeers of others. When Dickens died, leaving *The Mystery of Edwin Drood* only half done, he unleashed generations of armchair sleuths, quizzical amateurs, who've filled shelves with volumes purporting to explain who killed Drood and why. (Edmund Wilson called these explicators "Druids.") Spicer was a Dickensian and would have been pleased to provoke a similar response. We have thought hard and long about the clues left within the body of the text, and we believe we know "whodunit."

Beyond Druidical speculation, the hunt for a human soul is the most exciting thriller of all. Jim Ralston's return to the Bay Area, and his search for a new kind of poetry, amount to a pilgrimage, an unavailing hunt for an unreal Grail. His awkward involvement with Madelaine and his tentative exchange of powers with Rue Talcott bring him ambiguous pleasure, and result in a single new poem, at which point the novel ends. "Rue was now sitting on the bed crying. Ralston left." Why go on?

Or: how go on? Ralston's able to write only after (or in the act of) losing Rue's poetry, continuing the competition of their first meeting at The Birdcage, where each destroys the other's

---

*And a political allegory. The central question — "What time did Washington Jones leave the party?" is deliciously echoed by the question of "When did Slingbot (and Jones' attorney, Simpson) leave the Party?" Perhaps the Cold War theme would have been expanded, broadening the social aspects of the detective plot.

poem. In *The Tower of Babel*, poetry is superscription, a series
of cancellations and removals, like eighteenth-century corre-
spondence, on the slant. Anxiety of influence abounds, extend-
ing to the sexual. In their last scene together, Ralston is
"vaguely glad" Rue has put on his clothes. How go on? No
wonder the novel ends where it does. *The Tower of Babel*
illuminates beautifully, if fitfully, all that comes after. In his
next poem, *Billy the Kid* (1958), Spicer would take up the
sullen, thanatopic erotics Rue projects so strongly. And in the
"Homage to Creeley" section of *Heads of the Town up to the
Aether* (1960/61) and in *The Holy Grail* (1962), Spicer elaborat-
ed the theories of the kingship of poetry, the battle between
East and West, the rituals of obeisance and fealty, which he
had first learned at Berkeley from the medieval historian
Ernst Kantorovicz.

In this light the Slingbot/Madelaine/Ralston triangle is a
slangy, modern version of the Arthur/Gwenivere/Lancelot
story, the Camelot legend, which in turn corresponded to
Spicer's own feeling of expulsion from a lost Berkeley paradise.
This was a cluster of such great power that Spicer returned to
it again and again, each time extracting a grander formal
meaning, from satire (in the present piece) to allegory ("Homage to Creeley") to myth (*The Holy Grail*). While Madelaine is
wife, muse, mother, hostess, girlfriend, heroine, "prose writer,"
she's also a symbol of an enviable freedom from all these roles.
(She seems to lose a child as the story goes on, but that
doesn't dim her maternal determination.) As she takes center-
stage and assumes a vivid role of her own in the detective
"plot," her rueful, jaded monologues are sketches for those of
Gwenivere in Spicer's grail story.

So who killed Washington Jones, and why? Assume that
Jones was not killed by Sonia in a classic rape-revenge plot —
for surely this would be a little, well, *obvious*. Assume further,
as would most male readers of the fifties, either that no assault in fact occurred or that Jones was anyhow innocent,
Sonia either lying or mistaken — the stereotype of the *femme
fatale* so that Madelaine can somehow appear not to be one.
Assume that Ralston and Madelaine continue to run all
around San Francisco not only to imitate Nick and Nora
Charles but literally to uncover their object, the truth of

Washington Jones' alibi. Ergo, Jones was killed because of something he had seen during those "missing" hours. The rest is speculation, but we have our favorite suspects. Among them is Anne, Ralston's psychiatrist wife, the anti-Madelaine who's against poetry. What's to prevent Anne from flying in from Boston, committing a few crimes, and flying back? (Ralston never seems to be able to get her on the phone.) A stronger suspect is Rue, who might arguably have connived with Sonia to concoct a case against Jones, then panicked when the truth seemed to be getting the upper hand. If Ralston could prove *Rue* guilt of murder, the *Maltese Falcon* echoes, of deception and sexual betrayal, would be deafening. But why kill Jones, what was it Jones saw? What more ironic locum than an adulterous episode of Madelaine's?* (Perhaps with Rue, who seems familiar enough with her back stairs. Or how about Tom, the first husband conveniently lodged in New Mexico, but said to be off for the summer?) In this case little Janie's propensity for spying on her mother would no doubt have had an unpleasant, though salutary, result, had Spicer continued his tale, if it hadn't proved impossible. Wouldn't also that singular bottle of bismuth, introduced so cleverly so "casually," as Janie's unneeded "medicine," have played a part in the denouement, as another form of "green death"?†

But instead came *Billy the Kid* and all the other books. Five years later, in February 1963, Spicer's Los Angeles agency closed operations and returned him his manuscript. Much had changed since he had begun the novel in a burst of white heat. He was no longer talking to Robert Duncan, who had typed the ms. The Bohemians caricatured in the novel had dispersed, and a new crowd of poets surrounded Spicer at Gino & Carlo's bar nightly. The Berkeley Renaissance was even further away, remembered now only in scraps. And Spicer was in the middle of a prolonged creative slump that would not be re-

*Does this tie in, also, with the odd business about Madelaine's driver's license — the status of her marriage to Slingbot?

†We'd love to hear from proponents of other theories, or those who, like modern-day Charles Collinses, Luke Fildeses, were *there* when Spicer planned this novel.

lieved until the first poems of *Language* began to appear in November 1963. He put the novel away in his footlocker, closed the lid. In August 1965, after Spicer's death, Robin Blaser and Don Allen opened the footlocker at his family's bequest. On top of the typescript was a Zuni fetish, a hex or curse, pointing in the general direction of Duncan's house. In 1991 Robin Blaser gave us a typescript of the novel in support of our research on Jack Spicer's biography. In a Xerox shop near the University of British Columbia in Vancouver, he stood watchfully by, almost wistful, as page after page emerged from the machine into the "whole visible world."

— Lew Ellingham
Kevin Killian
San Francisco, November 1993

Designed by
Samuel Retsov

•

Text: 10 pt
New Century Schoolbook

•

acid-free paper

•

Printed by
McNaughton & Gunn, Inc.